'I don't think I want to work with you.'

He gave an [obscured] what you wou[ld]

'Yes.' She bit [obscured]

'And you can [obscured]

She stared into the depths of her glass. 'Not easily, no. I'm flattered, of course, but…'

'I wasn't looking to flatter you. I see you as someone with dedication and vision. Perhaps I was wrong, if you think of refusing for reasons which are strictly personal.' He looked at her over the rim of his glass and said huskily, 'Because you know that I find you beautiful. Does it trouble you, Beth? To know that I want you?'

She moistened her dry lips with her tongue. 'That isn't possible. You don't even know me.'

A muscle pulsed in his jaw. 'I know that you've been hurt. But you have to learn to let go, Beth,' he urged softly. 'I would never hurt you.'

Not intentionally, maybe, she thought.

Jean Evans was born in Leicester and married shortly before her seventeenth birthday. She has two married daughters and several grandchildren. She gains valuable information and background for her Medical Romances™ from her husband, who is a senior nursing administrator. She now lives in Hampshire, close to the New Forest and within easy reach of the historic city of Winchester.

Recent titles by the same author:

MOTHER ON CALL

DID YOU PURCHASE THIS BOOK WITHOUT A COVER?
If you did, you should be aware it is **stolen property** as it was reported *unsold and destroyed* by a retailer. Neither the author nor the publisher has received any payment for this book.

All the characters in this book have no existence outside the imagination of the author, and have no relation whatsoever to anyone bearing the same name or names. They are not even distantly inspired by any individual known or unknown to the author, and all the incidents are pure invention.

All Rights Reserved including the right of reproduction in whole or in part in any form. This edition is published by arrangement with Harlequin Enterprises II B.V. The text of this publication or any part thereof may not be reproduced or transmitted in any form or by any means, electronic or mechanical, including photocopying, recording, storage in an information retrieval system, or otherwise, without the written permission of the publisher.

This book is sold subject to the condition that it shall not, by way of trade or otherwise, be lent, resold, hired out or otherwise circulated without the prior consent of the publisher in any form of binding or cover other than that in which it is published and without a similar condition including this condition being imposed on the subsequent purchaser.

MILLS & BOON and MILLS & BOON with the Rose Device are registered trademarks of the publisher.

*First published in Great Britain 2003
Harlequin Mills & Boon Limited,
Eton House, 18-24 Paradise Road, Richmond, Surrey TW9 1SR*

© Jean Evans 2003

ISBN 0 263 83453 0

*Set in Times Roman 10½ on 12¼ pt.
03-0603-45296*

*Printed and bound in Spain
by Litografia Rosés, S.A., Barcelona*

HER ITALIAN DOCTOR

BY
JEAN EVANS

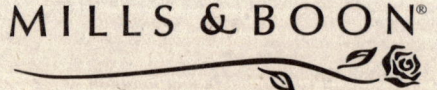
MILLS & BOON

CHAPTER ONE

'BETH, this is James.' The voice came urgently over the answering machine. 'Where the hell are you? I've been trying to reach you for the past twenty-four hours. Look, something's going on—something you should know about. Switch on your mobile. Get in touch. We really need to talk.'

Dr Beth Bryant's fingers drummed impatiently against the steering-wheel as yet another set of traffic lights changed to red—not that many of the other drivers seemed to notice, or even care.

'Oh, come on!' Naples traffic at any time of the day was chaotic, and mid-June temperatures soaring into the nineties were doing nothing to sweeten tempers, her own included. Even now, after almost three years, she had still not managed to adjust to the volatile Italian way of life. A scooter sounding like an angry wasp buzzed past, sagging beneath the weight of a family of three.

Beth took her hands off the wheel to lift the heavy swathe of honey-blonde hair from her neck, but the relief it brought was almost non-existent. The lights changed to green. Cars raced ahead, tyres screeching. The lights were red again. Behind her a shirtsleeved taxi driver had his radio playing at full blast. Beth reached across to the passenger seat for her briefcase, feeling hot and cross. It wasn't as if she knew *why* she was making this headlong dash across the city.

She thumbed through the pages of her diary, one eye warily on the traffic lights. This was her first day back after a spell of much-needed leave and she was due to discuss the hospital's half-yearly budget with Max, the senior medical director, and her other colleagues. She flipped the page. There was her regular rheumatology clinic later that morning and a couple of meetings—nothing else, apart from her usual duties. Nothing so urgent surely that it couldn't have waited until she arrived at her usual time.

Beth nibbled at her lower lip and turned to glare at the driver of the sports car that slid soundlessly alongside her own car. It really was too bad of James. Unlike him, too. His message had been cryptic to say the least. She wondered briefly what could have prompted it—wished he had been more specific as she let her gaze drift idly to the man in the car next to her.

It seemed unfair that anyone could look so cool and unruffled in such heat, especially in the expensively cut suit he was wearing. He stared straight ahead, giving a clear view of his profile, and Beth found herself staring at strong, chiselled features, a straight, classical nose and dark hair which, with the sun-bronzed complexion, made her aware that he was unquestionably Italian.

He turned his head slowly to look at her, and for several seconds Beth looked into thickly lashed, dark brown eyes which, at this moment, were filled with amusement.

With a quick intake of breath she looked away,

conscious, as her cheeks tinged with pink, that she had been staring and, worse, that for several seconds he had blatantly returned that look.

She fumbled with the gears, realising that the lights had changed to green, and suffered the ignominy of seeing the sports car glide ahead. The driver's hand rose mockingly in salute as he pulled away, leaving her struggling ahead of a line of impatient drivers, all blaring their horns.

'All right! I'm going.' Beth's mouth compressed as she found the right gear and sent the small car juddering forward into the mainstream of traffic.

Grinding her teeth, she stared purposefully ahead and didn't relax until she saw her turning. The Hermitage, a small privately funded hospital, was set back from the road. Manoeuvring the car out of the traffic, Beth drove through the open wrought-iron gates and came to a halt on the palm-shaded gravel drive.

Grabbing her bag and briefcase, she headed for the glass automatic doors, walked straight through the reception area and paused only briefly at the desk where the attractive young Italian receptionist reached out to answer the phone.

'*Pronto?* Ah, Signor Thomson. Yes, the doctor has had the results of your tests. If you would like to come in tomorrow he will see you then.' Replacing the receiver, she looked up and recognised Beth. 'Oh, Dottore Bryant. It's you. You're nice and early.'

Beth glanced at her watch. 'I got a call from Dr Sinclair, asking me to come in. It sounded rather urgent, so here I am.'

'Oh, *si*, of course. So you know, then?' Maria

Lazio shook her head sadly. 'It is all a very big shock. Dottore Sinclair is expecting you.'

Feeling slightly bemused, Beth thanked her. 'I take it he's in the staffroom.'

'No.' Maria swung to answer the phone again, cupping a neatly manicured hand over the receiver. 'The meeting finished half an hour ago. He's in his consulting room.'

'Damn!' Beth frowned. 'All right, thanks, Maria.' She turned and headed for the door, a tall, slender figure with grey-green eyes, a small, uptilted nose and a generous mouth which, at this moment, bore a hint of determination.

James's consulting room was at the end of a light, airy corridor, but she heard the raised voices long before she reached it. The door was ajar and she paused for a second, suddenly reluctant to intrude as she heard James's voice sharp with tension.

'So what the hell do you expect me to do? What *can* I do? I'm as shocked as everyone else about what's going on.'

'But surely you must have had some inkling? How could a thing like this happen so quickly, without warning?' Grace Hamilton, the senior nurse, sounded dangerously close to tears.

Smiling briefly at a young nurse who looked neat and cool in her short-sleeved white dress, Beth tapped firmly at the door and went in.

'Sorry to intrude, but the door was open.'

'Beth. Oh, thank heavens.' James stood up, his face a study of relief as he went to meet her, and it was easy to see why. Grace Hamilton's eyes held a distinct trace of tears.

She blew her nose hard. 'I'm sorry. I'm afraid I didn't see you there, Doctor.'

'I...er...I did knock.'

'It's OK.' James ran a hand wearily through his hair. 'You're not interrupting anything, certainly nothing that isn't common knowledge by now, anyway.'

'That's a joke.' Grace's laugh was bitter. 'I'm beginning to think I was the last person to see it coming.'

'Look, would someone mind telling me what's going on?' Beth looked from one to the other as she dropped her briefcase on the nearest chair. The windows were open and a warm breeze lightly fanned the curtains. 'I'd had a very nice leave until I got your message, James. And if I may say so, its content left a lot to be desired. Couldn't you have been a little more specific, instead of expecting me to drop everything and hare across town in this heat?'

'Yes, I'm sorry about that. Things have been going crazy here. Everything's moved faster than anyone expected.'

'I'd say that's the understatement of the year.' Grace threw him a scathing look. 'I feel as if I've been hit by a train.'

'Look,' Beth intervened hastily, 'I hate to break this up, but I still don't have a clue what's going on. I take it you didn't get me here just to act as a referee while you two slug it out.'

They both subsided, looking shamefaced, but it was James who spoke first. 'I don't quite know how to tell you this,' he said tersely.

'Why not try straight out?' Beth suggested. 'At least it might save time.'

James looked at her for a second then shrugged.

'We've been taken over. The whole hospital—all of it—lock, stock and barrel.' He got up from the desk where he had been half sitting. 'Our sponsors pulled out. I'm sorry, there's no easier way to put it.'

Beth stared at James for several seconds as his words failed to register, then, slowly, as if he had physically hit her, she reached for a chair and sat down.

'I—I'm sorry, I can't quite take this in. You're—you're not serious?'

'Oh, he's serious all right. It's true.' Grace flicked her a look. 'The staff were all summoned to a meeting first thing this morning and given the news. *Told*, mind you, not consulted. By the time we got to hear about it, the whole deal had been signed and delivered. We're now part of Medics International. It was a complete shock. Well, to most of us, anyway.' She turned away, her hands shaking as she fumbled for a fresh tissue.

Beth looked at James, almost too stunned to speak. 'Is it true?'

He dug his hands in the pockets of his lightweight suit. 'That's why I left the message. The directors called a meeting to break the news and we've been told to expect significant changes in the way the hospital is run. I reckoned you'd want to know what was happening.'

Beth swallowed hard. 'I'm still not sure I do understand, James.' Her eyes mirrored her confusion. 'How could it happen?'

James's face was grim. 'There's a lot of competition in the field of private medicine these days and we've been losing out. If we're honest, we've all seen it happening but we've done nothing about it.'

'Oh, come on, you can be more honest than that,' Grace said cuttingly. 'The whole place needs modernising. It needs money—serious money—spent on it.'

'I'm sure Max has done his best,' Beth challenged. 'He's worked damned hard since he took over as Medical Director ten years ago.' She broke off, frowning. 'Talking of which, where is he? What does he think of all this? He must be pretty shocked.'

'Max has gone, Beth.'

'Gone!' She stared at James and gave a slight laugh. 'Gone? You mean he's taken the day off? Well, I can't say I blame him.'

'Beth, that isn't what I'm saying. Max has gone. I understand he had a meeting with the hospital's sponsors a few days ago. He left shortly after and hasn't been seen since. All we know is what we've been told in a statement that was issued this morning saying that Dr Puigi has decided to take early retirement with immediate effect.'

Grace gave a harsh laugh. 'Well, I suppose that's one way of putting it. The question is, did he go or was he pushed, and what about the rest of us? Some of the staff have been here for years, it won't be easy to get new jobs. Or maybe they're planning to close the whole place down?'

'But they can't do that. Surely they wouldn't?' Beth looked from one to the other. 'I know image is important, but...' Beth's mouth suddenly felt very dry. 'But what will happen to the patients if we close? No one can fault the medical care we give. We all work so hard. Surely we at least have a right to know where we stand.'

'I brought that very point up at the meeting this morning, but no one was prepared to offer any reassurances at this stage. It looks as if the new owners call the shots, and until they do so we carry on.' He raked a hand through his hair. 'I don't know what's going to happen to any of us.'

'What about Nigel? How has he taken this? Where is he? Or has he gone, too?'

James shook his head. 'He's in Theatre. He's got a full operating list, including a spinal injury case that came in in the early hours. You know what it's like at this time of year. Peak holiday season. Tourists with a death wish.'

'Nigel is a top-class surgeon. Surely his job will be safe?'

'I imagine so. They'll always need surgeons.'

Beth got to her feet and went to stand at the window, staring out at the busy road. 'I still can't believe this is happening.' She turned to look at James. 'And what about all the ideas we've been discussing, about expanding some of the departments? I've been arguing for months that we need extra casualty facilities…a bigger rheumatology department…'

'Yes, well, now we know why they were always dragging their heels.' Grace looked pityingly at Beth's ashen face.

Beth pressed a hand shakily over her forehead. 'So, where do we stand with the new sponsors?'

'Your guess is as good as mine.'

'But…if Max has left, surely that means…' She glanced up at him, her face momentarily brightening. 'Won't you be in line for the medical director's job? Of course, I'm sad that Max has gone but I know you always expected…hoped…'

James gave a short laugh. 'It doesn't work that way, apparently. They're bringing in their own man.' He shifted uncomfortably.

'Does anyone know anything about him?'

'Not a lot.' James dug his hands in his pockets. 'His name is D'Angelo, but from the little I've heard it sounds as if he's the sort who deals strictly with percentages, not people.'

'D'Angelo?' Beth echoed hollowly.

'Nick D'Angelo,' Grace supplied caustically. 'Our new boss. I've never met him, but I've heard plenty. He's head hatchet man for Medics International. And when I say hatchet man, I mean hatchet man. Believe me, he doesn't waste any time. I wouldn't be surprised if the redundancy notices are already being prepared.'

'You're not serious?' Beth turned to look at James. 'Surely he can't do that?'

'Oh, take it from me,' Grace answered for him. 'Our Mr D'Angelo is an expert. He didn't even bother to show up for the meeting this morning but, then, he has people who do his dirty work for him, which apparently includes putting on hold any projects that may be in the pipeline.'

Beth flung a look at James. 'What about my research project—the funding?'

He gave a defeated shrug. 'I don't know. All I *do*

know is that the new sponsors want to take a look at everything.'

'But surely it must mean something, that people have worked at the hospital for years?'

Grace laughed scathingly. 'You don't imagine a man like that has a conscience. He'll do what the sponsors tell him to do.'

'Oh, come on, Grace,' James intervened sharply. 'This is business, not personal, and we're not solving anything like this.'

'Maybe not.' She rounded on him. 'But, then, you're not out of a job—yet.'

Someone tapped at the door and one of the nurses popped her head round. 'Oh, Sister, I'm sorry to bother you, but Mr Benson is complaining of stomach pains again. I wonder if you'd take a look at him?'

'I'll be right there.' She nodded and the nurse hurried away.

Beth's gaze flew from one to the other in questioning disbelief. 'You don't mean... Oh, surely not...'

Grace's mouth twisted. 'As good as. Oh, I've been told there's a senior sister's job at one of the company's other hospitals, but it's hardly going to be the same, is it?'

James's mouth tightened. 'At least don't dismiss the offer out of hand.'

'Well, that's easy to say—you're not the one being asked to move. I've got a good nursing team here. We work well together.' Grace smiled bleakly at Beth. 'Look, I'm sorry about this. I'm afraid it's been one of those days, and thanks to Mr D'Angelo I doubt if my life will ever be quite the same again.' She reached for her bag and headed for the door. 'I have a patient on renal dialysis. I need to check how he's getting on. After that I may go and have several very strong coffees, and if anyone wants me, frankly, right now I don't give a damn.' She looked at Beth. 'Perhaps we can talk later, when I've had time to calm down.'

Beth nodded. 'I'd like that.'

James pushed the door closed behind Grace and went to sit heavily in the chair behind the desk. 'She's obviously a bit uptight.'

Beth gave a laugh of incredulity. 'Well, quite honestly, James, I can't say I blame her. I'm feeling more than a little uptight myself right now.' She paced to the window and back, her movements unconsciously graceful in spite of her agitation. 'I still don't understand how this could happen. When I think of Max, and…and all his hard work.'

James seemed to find her anger embarrassing. 'Maybe I should have tried to warn you earlier, when I first heard the rumours, but that's all they were. I didn't believe it would happen, or that D'Angelo would be quite as ruthless.' He got to his feet and went to put his arms round her. 'I'm sorry, sweetheart. I feel damned guilty.'

Beth frowned at a thought too fleeting even to grasp, then shook her head as she turned in the circle of his arms. 'I feel so frustrated, so angry. You don't suppose they'll actually close us down? They wouldn't, would they? Not when we've all worked so hard. We're needed here.'

James traced the line of her cheek and throat, and her response was purely instinctive as his mouth came down on hers.

Her relationship with James had developed slowly over the past couple of years, on her part at least. She had guessed almost from the beginning that his own interest in her was more physical, of course, but she had been too unsure of her own feelings—still was, for that matter—to let it develop beyond the occasional date and a few kisses.

'Things may not be as bad as they seem right now,' James murmured into her hair. 'You'll be all right, Beth. You're a great doctor.'

She wasn't fooled by the attempt at reassurance. 'Let's face it, as far as the new sponsors are concerned, I'm just one small fish in a tiny pool. There are lots of good doctors who'd be only too happy to work out here in Italy, and who could blame them? I sometimes think we have the best of all worlds—doing a job we love, almost permanent sunshine.' She frowned. 'I don't know how I'd cope with having to go back to England, starting all over again.' Her mouth twisted. 'One thing's for sure, though, I'd give anything to meet the man face to face, just to see what sort of arrogant bastard it is who plays with other people's lives like this.' Her cheeks flushed. 'I'd like to tell Signor Nick D'Angelo precisely what I think of him.'

'I'm sure I'd find the experience most enlightening.'

At the sound of the voice coming from behind her, Beth spun round, her attention riveted on the man standing in the doorway, and felt as if an electric current had passed through her body.

It wasn't just the overwhelming sense of power and self-assurance which seemed to emanate from him as he stood there, though that in itself was sufficient to send a shiver of awareness running down her spine. It was something in the deep, dark eyes which raked her slender figure and delicate features with an intensity so vibrantly sexual that it almost took her breath away.

He came slowly into the room, tall, slim and muscular, so that she was immediately conscious of every line, from the taut shoulders to a slim waist and lean thighs beneath the dark trousers he was wearing. She was also aware, as the flush darkened in her cheeks, that she had seen this man before, that morning, driving the sports car. Even as the velvet brown eyes bored deeply into hers she knew, with a terrible sinking feeling, that this was Nick D'Angelo.

With a determined effort, she dragged her gaze up to meet his. 'You!' She moistened her suddenly dry lips and his gaze narrowed, as if to mock what he knew to be an air of assumed self-confidence.

Humour glinted in his eyes. 'Dare I say we must stop meeting like this?'

Beth's throat felt painfully tight. Seen close to, the black hair was even darker than she had imagined, longer, too, as it curled slightly over the collar of his blue shirt.

She swallowed hard. 'It might be a little corny, don't you think?'

James hovered uncomfortably. 'Am I to take it that you two know each other?'

Nick D'Angelo gave a husky laugh, showing teeth which looked startlingly white against the deeply tanned features.

'That may be putting it a little strongly.' The narrow gaze was directed straight at Beth, and she felt her blush deepen. 'You could say we were more like ships that pass in the night, except that, unlike most such encounters, ours is becoming increasingly intriguing.'

Beth almost choked with embarrassment. Her chin rose.

'I take it you *are* Signor D'Angelo? In which case, I suppose I owe you an apology. You weren't supposed to overhear.'

'No?' The dark eyebrows rose and she found herself subjected to a flagrantly masculine appraisal as his gaze swept over her. 'But, then, they do say listeners never hear anything good of themselves. Isn't that so?'

'Obviously they are right,' she shot at him sweetly, and intercepted a quelling look from James.

'Signor D'Angelo, this is Dr Bryant, Beth Bryant, and, despite what you may think, it wasn't quite the way it may have seemed. It was a mistake, a misunderstanding.'

Beth's eyes flashed dark green. 'I don't need you to make excuses for me, James. Please, don't get involved. I'm quite capable of fighting my own battles.'

'Ah. I must try to remember that.' Nick D'Angelo's voice was a soft drawl, and Beth wished she could back away from the tantalising smell of expensive aftershave as he moved imperceptibly closer.

She flicked him a glance. Was he being funny? Everything about this man, from the tall, tautly muscled physique to the arrogant good looks, spelt sex appeal. There was no denying that Nick D'Angelo had the kind of looks that would appeal to most women—except herself, she thought decisively. He wasn't her type and, anyway, right now she wasn't interested.

She met his gaze directly. 'I'm sure you'll want me to speak honestly. I've been hearing about the sort of tactics you use, and frankly I don't care for them. I don't suppose it matters to you that you might be wrecking people's lives.'

'For heaven's sake, Beth!' James's face was white. 'You don't know what you're saying.'

She shook him off, aware of Nick D'Angelo watching her, his face without expression. 'I know exactly what I'm saying and so, I think, does Mr D'Angelo.' She waited warily. He looked far too calm. 'At least you'll note he hasn't bothered to deny it. Now, why is that, do you suppose? Could it be because he knows it's true?'

Nick D'Angelo frowned. His gaze swept to James. He walked to the door, opening it. 'Perhaps you'd like to leave us alone for a while, Dr Sinclair.'

With one tense look in her direction, James went— leaving her to face Nick D'Angelo alone. He studied her, taking in the firm set of her mouth, the truculence in the taut angle of her jaw, before he moved to stand with his hands in his pockets.

'You're upset, *signorina*.'

'Upset!' Her head jerked up and she gave a short laugh. 'Yes, I think you could say I'm upset. And it's *signora*, by the way. *Mrs* Bryant, not miss. Max is hardly out of the door and you walk in as if...as if...'

'As if I own the place?' He supplied the words for her.

Beth almost choked. 'As I understand it, the fact is

that people may lose their jobs, but, then, I doubt if that's even a consideration, is it, Mr D'Angelo? Nor the fact that I've worked on my research project into Still's disease for the past two years, and now I hear the project may be put on hold, even though I was promised funding.' She tossed her head, looking at him.

He didn't move. Instead, he gave her a long searching look which sent the colour rushing into her cheeks.

'Actually, it's *Dr* D'Angelo,' he said evenly. His dark brows drew together. 'I can understand that you might resent someone coming in to take Max's place. I admire your loyalty, but let's get a few things straight, shall we? In the first place, I did not drive Max out. It was *his* decision. He chose to go.'

'I don't believe you. Max loved his work.'

'And his work was much respected. But in spite of what you think, it *was* his decision.'

'Oh, I see. And it was simply a matter of perfect timing that he *chose* to go just as you arrived on the scene, ready to step into his shoes.'

A muscle flicked in his jaw. 'I can see that it must seem so.'

She drew a ragged breath. 'Max lived for his work here at the hospital. It was his life.'

'Not quite his life. Max was under a lot of pressure recently.'

'Pressure goes with the job. Max knew that. He was a fine doctor—one of the best.'

'You don't have to tell me about his reputation. It is well known.' He looked at her and frowned. 'There's something you obviously don't know. I have no wish to betray a confidence but since we have to work together, you and I, I think we shall only do so amicably if we can trust each other.'

'I don't understand,' Beth said tautly. 'What are you trying to say?'

'You know that Max has a daughter?'

'Yes, of course—Sophia. She's married to an American doctor. They went to live in the States.'

He nodded. 'She's in hospital.'

Beth felt suddenly cold. 'I... What happened?'

'I understand she has meningitis.'

Beth felt her throat tighten. 'Oh, no. She's not...?'

'No. She is very ill, but I understand that she is responding to medication. Obviously Max and his wife want to be with her.'

She expelled a harsh breath. 'Yes, of course they do. But... Why didn't Max say anything?'

'Because there were things to be arranged in a hurry and he didn't want a fuss. They both just want to be with their daughter. He spoke to the new sponsors, of course. Obviously they had to be told. He would have been due to retire in eighteen months anyway. He wanted to go now, and it made sense.'

Beth took a deep breath. 'I wish I'd known. I might have been able to do something.'

'Like what? You have no reason to feel guilty or to reproach yourself.'

'Haven't I?' she asked tautly. 'Max has been a good friend. He was always there for me when...' She broke off and drew herself to look at him, and for a few crazy seconds was suddenly, disconcertingly aware of Nick D'Angelo as a man, and a very attractive man at that. Until now she hadn't noticed the tiny lines of tiredness edging his mouth, but they were there, adding a kind of harshness which momentarily left her feeling vaguely shaky.

Colour flooded her face as with a start she jerked back to the realisation that he was speaking.

'I...I'm sorry?'

'I was saying that this is not the way I would have wished it. But we all owe it to Max to make things work, don't you think? Medicine changes. Times change. Patients expect—have a right to expect that the treatment they receive will be the best.' His mouth twisted. 'I realise that profit may seem like a dirty word but it is a necessary evil if we are to update equipment and facilities.' He frowned. 'I realise that Max will be a hard act to follow, but I shall do my best. I don't expect it to be easy.'

'Well, I suppose that's something at least.'

His eyes met hers. 'I want us to be able to work together, and that will be easier if I have your support. This hospital needs someone who is prepared to give one hundred percent commitment. I promise you that for as long as I'm here that's what I'll give, and I expect everyone else to do the same. I don't want a fight.'

'What's the matter? Afraid of losing, Doctor?'

He straightened up and she saw the look of cool amusement in his eyes. 'Oh, I rarely lose, Dr Bryant,' he said softly. 'But, then, that's something you have yet to learn about me. I don't underestimate the amount of work to be done. I'll do whatever it takes, and that includes making decisions which I know may not be popular. In the meantime, I'd like to think we can at least be friends.'

She gave a slight laugh. 'Friendship has to be earned, Doctor.'

'True.' He smiled. 'We seem to have got off to a bad start. I'm sorry about that. It isn't easy, stepping into someone else's shoes, especially when that someone is well liked and respected. But somehow we have to make it work.'

Beth looked at him and swallowed hard. 'So, what exactly are you suggesting?'

His mouth twisted. 'You could start by calling me Nick.'

She tested the sound and found it surprisingly pleasant. 'All right—Nick.'

Humour glinted in his eyes. 'There, that wasn't so difficult, was it? So, I take it, then, that I can count on your full co-operation?'

Her breath snagged in her throat. Too much coffee, she told herself sharply. 'I beg your pardon?'

Brown eyes glinted. 'Professionally speaking, of course.' He straightened up. 'So, tell me, *signora*, what made you decide to come to Italy? Is your husband also a doctor? Is that how you met?'

Beth felt her heart give a painful thud. She closed her eyes briefly, breathing deeply as she felt herself falling into the grey, suffocating mists of the old, familiar nightmare. In her mind's eye she saw it happening all over again. Paul...the car...the policeman arriving to tell her there had been an accident, and after that the pain and guilt, and then the numbness of both mind and body which had made living more bearable—until now, when this total stranger had unknowingly but none the less savagely reopened the wound.

She opened her eyes to look at him and said raggedly, 'My husband was killed in a car accident four years ago. Does that satisfy your curiosity, or perhaps you'd like to ask questions?'

For an instant a look of compassion filled his eyes, then he shook his head. 'So you came to Italy to escape?'

'I came to work. I needed a change of direction, to get away, but I've loved Italy ever since my parents brought me here as a child. So when the opportunity arose to work at this hospital I took it.'

'Four years is a long time for anyone to grieve with such intensity.'

Her green eyes flashed. 'Why? Are you saying that because I'm a doctor I should be immune to real emotions? Well, I'm afraid it doesn't work that way. This was personal.' She brushed a hand fleetingly against her forehead. 'You've changed the subject. This isn't about me, it's about what is going to happen here. I still don't understand how any of this could have happened. Why were we kept in the dark? Why was it all kept so quiet?'

'It wasn't.'

'Oh, come on. You don't expect me to believe that?'

He moved to sit on the edge of the desk and said evenly, 'I'm telling you the facts, which I assume you could just as easily get from Dr Sinclair. The possibility of a change of ownership was first mooted a couple of months ago. Admittedly it wasn't shouted from the rooftops. I don't know what your relationship with Sinclair is, but it must have struck you that as one of the senior doctors here he could have kept you in the picture more.'

'There is no relationship, Doctor.'

'But not for any lack of enthusiasm on his part, I dare say. Any man would be a fool not to be captivated.' The dark eyes studied her flushed cheeks, and she drew a long, steadying breath.

'Let's leave James out of this, shall we? Tell me what will happen to this hospital, to the people who work here, when you start making your changes?'

'Nothing's been decided yet.'

'But—'

He said softly, 'I'm not responsible for the rumours, Beth. Until I've had a chance to look at the situation I can't give you the answers you want.' He looked at her. 'You mentioned your research project. Tell me, why Still's disease? That's juvenile arthritis, isn't it?'

'Yes, it is. My sister was diagnosed with the condition at the age of ten. She was in a lot of pain.' She tucked a strand of hair behind her ear in a nervous gesture. 'It seemed so unfair. Most people associate arthritis with an older age group. I suppose I've always wanted to know why it happened to Julie. I wanted to know what triggers the condition, what can be done to alleviate it, why people respond to different drug regimes. I'm not looking for sympathy. Julie wouldn't…'

'I'm not offering any,' he said softly. 'Is that why you chose medicine as a career?'

'It seemed the natural thing to do. I don't remember ever considering anything else. I just wanted to go to medical school.' Her mouth curved into an involuntary smile. 'It was a bit like…like coming home. I knew I'd made the right decision.'

'Is that where you met your husband—in medical school?'

She jerked her head up, shocked by the realisation that he had somehow sensed her vulnerability, and resenting the intrusion. 'Yes, that's where I met Paul.' She turned to look at him and suddenly the pain was back again, the barriers were coming up, holding back the memories. Her fingers trailed over the surface of the desk, then went to her mouth, feeling it tremble. 'He was a brilliant doctor. He loved working in a hospital environment.'

'And you didn't?'

Again his perception took her by surprise. 'I prefer general practice. I enjoy getting to know my patients. I always felt there was something…impersonal about working in the hospital where patients came and went. We saw them maybe once. It was a bit like a conveyor belt. Paul was ambitious. I wasn't. I… Well, I loved what I was doing, helping people, hopefully making them better and being there to see an end result.' She flicked him a glance. 'I suppose that sounds very naïve.'

'Not at all. Why should it? So, how long were you married before the accident?'

She moistened her dry lips with her tongue. This was private territory and she was beginning to feel angry. 'Almost two years.'

'Sometimes it helps to talk, even to a stranger, and four years is a long time to bottle up so much grief. Life has to go on. You can't shut yourself away for ever and pretend it isn't happening.'

'What I do with my private life is none of your business.' Her face was pale as she met his gaze. 'And frankly, Doctor, I don't care to discuss my marriage with you.'

His gaze narrowed. 'Dreams make poor bedfellows, *cara*. You're very young. Life moves on. *You* have to move on. Unless, of course, you're afraid.' He glanced at his watch. 'Yes, well, I must get on. I'll see you in the morning, Doctor. As I said, we must talk, but right now I have to meet with some of our new sponsors who wish to take a tour of the hospital.'

Without waiting to see the effect his words had, Nick D'Angelo turned on his heel and walked away.

Beth's mouth tightened. Well, really! The man was too arrogant for words. It was galling to discover that her hands were actually shaking as she opened the door. This was ridiculous! She only had to work with the man, she didn't have to like him. So what was it about Nick D'Angelo that was making her so irrationally edgy?

Breathing hard, she marched briskly through to Reception and collected the day's mail. She felt confused by emotions she had no intention of recognising. It had been a long time since any man had roused anything more than indifference in her, and that was the way she preferred to keep it. Nick D'Angelo was the kind of experience she could well do without. As for seeing him again, it might be inevitable but she would make sure it didn't happen a moment sooner than it had to. As far as she was concerned, memories were far safer than the real thing.

CHAPTER TWO

THE phone was ringing insistently when Beth walked into her consulting room next morning. There was nothing unusual about it. With an ever-expanding contingent of British expatriates living in the area, not to mention a large local community, the hospital was often stretched to capacity.

Today, however, for some totally illogical reason, the sound of the phone ringing brought a rush of panic which made her hesitate in the doorway as she waited for it to stop. Only when it fell silent as Maria intercepted the call could she bring herself to walk into the room. Then, having hung up her jacket and flicked a comb through her hair, she walked through to the reception desk.

'Oh, Dottore Bryant. *Bon giorno*. I didn't see you come in. There was a call...'

'Don't worry about it.' Beth smiled. 'I won't be in my room for a while but if anything crops up, take a message and say I'll get back to whoever it is, will you? Or you can bleep me if it's urgent, of course.'

'*Si, Dottore.*'

'Thanks, Maria. By the way, I was just walking into my room as the phone stopped ringing.' She bit her lip, despising herself for the lie. 'I don't suppose you know who it was?'

'Oh, yes, that was Dottore Sinclair. Shall I get him back for you?'

For a second Beth almost laughed aloud at her own groundless fears as a surge of relief ran through her. 'Yes, please, Maria. Do that now, will you? Then I must do my ward round, so no more calls unless it is urgent, no matter who.'

'*Si*. Don't worry. I'll see to it.'

Beth returned to her consulting room and sat at her desk, aware that her hands were shaking. It was illogical, she knew, but the mere thought of crossing swords again so soon with Nick D'Angelo was more than she felt able to handle right now.

The phone rang, making her heart leap. 'Yes, Maria?'

'I have Dottore Sinclair for you.'

Beth had to clear her throat before her voice could come out. 'Thank you, Maria. Put him through.'

James's voice, familiar and tense, sounded in her ear. She smiled to herself, her equilibrium restored. She listened, reaching for a buff file containing a batch of typed letters which were awaiting signature.

Frowning, she fumbled in her pocket for a pen. 'James, I thought this was your day off. Yes. Yes... I've already said I don't blame you. No, of course I'm not angry with you. Why should I be?' She frowned, impatiently tucking the phone under her chin as she glanced at the first letter before signing it.

'Yes, yes, I know your hands were tied. I appreciate that. You only did what you had to do. The staff had to be told. The important thing is what happens next. No one likes being kept in the dark but, whether we like it or not, the new sponsors—and Dr D'Angelo, as the new medical director—call the shots right now. It was good of you to alert me to what's happening.'

Beth's friend, physiotherapist Emma Dawson, had tiptoed into the room to put a stack of files on the desk, and was on her way out when Beth gestured, mouthing at her to stay. 'Yes, James, I'd love to have dinner with you one evening, but not this week. No, no, I've said I'm not annoyed, but I do have a lot of catching up to do. Yes, that would be fine. Give me a call then. Yes, I'll look forward to it.' She put the phone down, sighing heavily.

'I take it that was James?' Emma perched herself on the desk. 'Giving you trouble, is he?'

'Not James! Just his conscience.' Beth pushed the letters away and raked a hand through her hair. 'Lord, what a mess! I've tried telling him he can't be held responsible. I mean, no one could have foreseen that Max would leave. Heaven knows, without James I might just have walked back into the whole thing without any warning.'

'You obviously haven't seen this.' Emma dropped a copy of the local newspaper on to the desk. 'There's a large piece about the hospital. It's all in there. Large international medical corporation takes over The Hermitage with a view to complete modernisation. You'd think they were opening a new health club,' she joked. 'Come to think of it, it might not be such a bad idea at that. I'd be one of the first to join, if I could afford it.' She turned the pages of the paper, folding it in half. 'There's a picture of our new medical director. He's quite a hunk, isn't he? Wow, just think! All that power and rich with it, and he can't be a day over thirty-five. What do you reckon?'

Beth stared at the unsmiling picture of Nick D'Angelo and felt her pulse quicken irrationally. Poor quality though the photograph was, there could be no mistaking those arrogant looks, the tanned face, the dark eyes and sensual mouth which, even from the page, seemed to mock her. She pushed the paper aside. 'Yes, well, I'm sure his rich friends will appreciate his efforts on their behalf. Frankly, he's not my type.'

'The trouble with you—' Emma eyed her sadly '—is that you're judging all men by Paul.' She saw the faint flush gather in her friend's cheeks, and deliberately chose to ignore it. 'I think you're scared you might meet someone who *is* your type, so you freeze them all out just to be on the safe side. And don't tell me to mind my own business, I've heard it before. I just happen to think it's a hell of a waste, that's all.'

Beth pressed a hand to her temple. 'Please, Emma, not now.'

'All right. But I've known you for a long time, and all I want is to see you making at least some effort to live again. It makes me so damned angry to see you filling your life with nothing but work when there are gorgeous hunks like this around for the taking.'

Beth's eyes flashed a warning. 'Right now my work is all I want. I don't need anything else. Certainly I don't need another man in my life, so can we drop the subject? And talking of work…' she rose to her feet and looked at her watch '…I don't know about you but I have patients to see. We are still open for business, regardless of what Dr D'Angelo may have in store for the future.'

'OK. I'm on my way.' Emma grinned as she headed for the door. 'See you later maybe for a coffee. I take it you will take a break some time?'

Beth gave an exasperated laugh. 'I'll see you. Now, do me a favour and just go.'

Five minutes later she walked in to a small side ward, smiling as she gently reached out to hold the wrist of the eighteen-year-old who was lying in the bed. 'So, how are you feeling today, Gary?' Her fingers registered his pulse. 'You're certainly looking a little less colourful.'

Gary Watson grinned sheepishly as he looked at his sun-reddened arms and chest. 'I'm feeling a lot better, thanks, Doc. Still a bit sore, mind.'

'Well, I'm not surprised. Let me take a look at your feet. Hmm, not a pretty sight, are they? But at least the swelling has gone down. With a bit of luck you might even be able to get your shoes on.'

'Does that mean I can go back to the hotel and join my mates? It's not been much of a holiday so far, stuck in this bed.'

'You were jolly lucky, you know.' Beth made a note on the clipboard before returning it to the end of the bed. 'You were in a pretty bad state by the time your friends got you to the hospital. Didn't anyone warn you about lying in the sun, especially at midday when it's at its hottest?' she chided gently.

'Yeah—well, I didn't mean to, did I?' Gary pushed back the sheet. 'Trouble was, we'd been out clubbing the night before—didn't get back to the hotel till nearly three in the morning. We went down to the pool a few hours later. I thought a dip might wake me up a bit, but I sat on one of the sunbeds afterwards, and next thing I knew I was in here.'

'Nicely fried to a crisp and with a temperature of a hundred and one.'

'I remember throwing up.'

'Nice one.' Beth grinned and shook her head. 'I just hope you've learned a lesson, that's all.'

'Oh, I won't be doing it again in a hurry, I can promise you that. So...when can I get out of here?' He frowned. 'Hey, my insurance *will* pay for this, won't it? I mean, this place doesn't come cheap. I only brought spending money and not too much of that.'

'Yes, don't worry. Our staff have been in contact with your holiday rep and it's all taken care of.'

'Great. So when can I go? I've still got a week of my holiday left. I'd like to make the most of it.'

Beth checked the areas of redness on his ears and nose before answering. 'Are the burns still painful?'

'No, not much.'

She nodded. 'In that case, I don't see any reason why you can't leave today.'

'Yeah! Great!' He punched a fist in the air.

'On one condition,' she said sternly. 'You cover up if you're going out in the sun. Wear a loose shirt and a hat. *And*—' Beth deliberately emphasised the word '—use a high-factor sunscreen and remember to keep reapplying it, especially if you go for a swim. You do know that constant exposure to the sun can cause skin cancer?'

'I'd heard, but, well, I mean, you don't think about it, do you?'

'Well, maybe it's time you did,' Beth said quietly,

then she smiled. 'I'll give you some more painkillers to take with you when you leave. You've still one or two blisters. A light coating of petroleum jelly should prevent anything sticking to them.'

'I can go, then?' He was already getting out of bed.

She gave a short laugh. 'Yes, you can go. I wouldn't want to keep you from your mates. Enjoy the rest of your holiday. I hope we don't see you again.'

'No chance.' Gary grinned. He was already reaching for his clothes.

With a wave of her hand, Beth left him to it. She was heading along the cool, airy corridor when Staff Nurse Maggie Thomas caught up with her. 'Hi. Have you got a minute?'

'Sure.' Beth glanced at her watch and smiled. 'What can I do for you?'

'I wonder if you could take a look at an elderly gentleman for me? He's seventy-two.' Maggie flipped through her notes. 'His wife brought him in to Accident and Emergency. They live locally, moved out here about five years ago after he retired. They thought a bit of sun might do them good.'

'Can't say I blame them. What's the problem?'

'Well, he's complaining of flu-like symptoms, but he also has pain.'

'Abdominal pain?'

'No, more in the region of his ribs.' Dark-haired, slim and attractive, Maggie matched her steps to Beth's as they walked towards the examination room. 'To tell you the truth, I'm having trouble getting any information out of him. I think he's scared. He did admit he'd been getting what he insists is indigestion, but I wonder if he's afraid it's something more serious. His wife is pretty anxious.'

'I imagine she would be. Right, let's take a look at him, then. Are those his details?'

'Such as they are.' Maggie handed them over. 'His name is Harry, by the way. Harry Simpson. His wife's name is Betty.'

'OK. So, let's take a look at him.'

Harry Simpson was sitting on the examination couch in one of the brightly curtained cubicles. His wife sat in a chair, holding his hand.

Beth smiled. 'Hello, Mr Simpson, Mrs Simpson. I'm Dr Bryant.' She glanced at the notes and looked at the man, noting the faint signs of jaundice which made the whites of his eyes look yellow. 'I gather you're not feeling too well.'

Harry drew himself up, winced and pressed a hand to his right side. 'It's probably something I've eaten. I don't want to make a fuss.'

'Harry, it's gone on too long, you've got to get it sorted.'

'How long, Mrs Simpson?' Beth glanced at the woman and reached for the man's wrist. She checked his pulse, noting at the same time that his skin also had a dusky yellow tinge.

'It's been weeks, on and off.'

Beth nodded. 'Can you show me exactly where the pain is, Mr Simpson?'

'Aye, it's here.' He pressed a hand just below his right ribs. 'And sometimes it's here.' His hand shifted to an area on his back, near the shoulder blade.

'Right. Look, lie down on the couch, make yourself comfortable and I'll make a quick examination.

That's fine. Try to relax.' She pressed gently below his ribs and Harry grunted. 'That's painful, is it?' She straightened up. 'When exactly do you get the pain?'

'After I've eaten. Indigestion, too.'

Beth made several notes. 'Have you given us a urine sample?'

'He did. I've checked it,' Maggie said, handing the small specimen bottle to Beth. The sample was very dark.

'So, what's the matter with me, Doctor? Can you do anything about it? I hate feeling like this. It's really beginning to get me down.'

'I'm sure it must be,' Beth said sympathetically. 'Well, all the signs are that you have gallstones. They are, literally, like small stones or pieces of gravel, but they aren't as hard. They're usually made up of cholesterol, which is a type of fat. Sometimes they block the tubes that drain the gall bladder, causing inflammation, or they move out of the gall bladder and block the tube leading to the intestine. That's what causes the jaundice and a fever, and sometimes severe colic. I'm pretty sure that's what has happened in your case, so I'm not surprised you're feeling poorly.'

'Can you do anything about it?'

'I certainly hope so.' Beth smiled. 'What I'd like to do now is to admit you so that we can do some tests.'

Betty Simpson's grip tightened on her husband's hand. 'What sort of tests?'

'We'll need to do a blood test to check your husband's liver, and we'll probably want to do an ultrasound scan which will show us whether you do have gallstones. It's quite painless. You'll just feel a slight pressure on your skin, and we'll be able to see a picture of your gall bladder on a monitor.'

'And if it is gallstones, what then?'

'If your gall bladder is inflamed you'll need to stay in hospital for a few days so that we can give you antibiotics via a drip. If there are any stones then I'd recommend that we operate to remove them.'

'An operation!' Betty Simpson's voice wavered.

'These days it's usually done by laparoscopic surgery—that is, keyhole surgery—and it means you'll only need to stay with us for a couple of nights, although naturally you'll need to come back for a check-up and to have the stitches removed. One thing I can promise you, you'll feel a whole lot better when it's sorted out. Look, I'll leave you to have a chat, then Staff Nurse here will come back and talk to you and take a few details. Then we'll take it from there, shall we?'

Half an hour later, having seen her last patient of the morning, Beth was heading for the staffroom and a welcome cup of coffee.

Emma was already installed in a chair, cup in hand as she flipped through the pages of a medical journal.

'You made it! I was beginning to think I'd missed you.' She grinned. 'I suppose this means I have to share the chocolate biscuits.'

'They're all yours.' Beth sank into a chair, stifling a jaw-cracking yawn before helping herself to coffee. 'This is what I need. Mmm, that's good.'

'Busy morning?'

'Just the usual.' Beth pulled a wry face. 'It's never easy, coming back after a few days' leave, is it?'

'How's Guiseppina, then, and that gorgeous husband of hers? What's his name?'

'Paulo.'

'Paulo.' Emma smiled. 'And that gorgeous baby of theirs. I remember now, they asked you to be her godmother, didn't they?'

'That's right. That's why I went up there for a couple of days. She's beautiful. They've called her Angelina, and she is just perfect.'

'Lucky people.'

'Yes, they are, and they know it.'

'I suppose the whole family turned out for the event?'

Beth laughed. 'You can say that again. Uncles, aunts, cousins, grandparents. It was wonderful. Eating outdoors in the shade of the olive trees—wine, marvellous food…'

'Oh, for heaven's sake, do shut up. I'm already green with envy *and* I'm supposed to be on a diet.' Emma sighed heavily. 'It's no good, I shall just have to have another biscuit after all.'

'You're impossible.' Beth smiled, glancing up as Maria came into the staffroom with a bundle of letters.

'Ah, *Dottore*, I was hoping I would find you. These are for you. Oh, and I know you said not to put any calls through, but one caller has been very persistent. I did tell him that you were very busy, and explained that I would take a message if it was urgent, but he refused. He has rung back several times and asked to speak to you in person.'

Beth's hand shook as she poured fresh coffee, exclaiming crossly as she spilled some in the saucer. 'Did he leave a name, or a number?'

'No, *Dottore*.' Maria screwed up her face apologetically. 'He just said that you'd know who it was, and that he does not give up easily. I'm sorry if that does not make sense. I did try.'

Beth's green eyes held a hint of panic. 'That's all right, Maria. I know you did.' She carefully avoided Emma's curious glance.

'So, what do you wish me to say if…when he calls again, *Dottore*?'

Several things sprang instantly to mind, but Beth suppressed the desire to voice them aloud. 'Just tell him the same as before, please, Maria—that I'm very busy and cannot be disturbed unless it is very urgent.'

'*Si, Dottore*. I did tell him that the last time he called.' She bit her lip apprehensively.

'And what did he say?'

'He says he keep trying till he gets you.'

'Oh, did he indeed?' Beth's face burned scarlet, and Emma choked over her coffee.

'Do I take it this is the rich and extremely handsome Dr D'Angelo? If so, you certainly have to give him full marks for persistence.'

Beth's mouth compressed ominously. 'Next time he calls, Maria, tell him I'm unavailable. Tell him…tell him Dr Sinclair can answer any of his questions.'

'Yes, *Dottore*.' Maria left the staffroom and Emma sat forward, her hands clasped round her cup of coffee. 'Look, I don't want to interfere, but aren't you taking this all a bit too seriously? I mean, what have you got against the man? Sooner or later you're going to have to talk to him. You're going to have to *work* with him and, let's face it, Beth, he does hold all the cards.'

'He obviously likes to think he does.' Beth threw her friend a slanting glance. Taking her coffee, she went to stand at the window, schooling her features to remain calm while inside her emotions were in turmoil.

For some reason she couldn't or didn't want to understand, Nick D'Angelo seemed to offer a threat. It had taken her four years to get her life back into some sort of order since Paul had died, and now, suddenly, it all seemed to be in jeopardy.

Her hand shook slightly as the pain of carefully submerged memories began bubbling up to the surface. Her work had helped. She had driven herself hard, almost to the point at one stage where her friends and colleagues had feared she'd been heading for a nervous breakdown.

They had all put it down to the accident, the shock of being told that Paul had been killed outright in the car that night when he had apparently skidded off the road and hit a tree. She hadn't attempted to disillusion them, but there had been more to it than that, Beth knew. Much more. Things she could never bring herself to talk about, not even to Emma who was her closest friend and ally.

And now, just when it seemed she had begun to get things back into some sort of perspective, see some purpose in what she was doing, Nick D'Angelo had come striding into her life and somehow managed to force a tiny gap in all her carefully erected barriers.

Well, barriers could be rebuilt, and she had no intention of allowing him to encroach any further.

'I have a job to do. I'm good at my job,' she said defensively. 'I don't need the precious Dr D'Angelo to tell me how to do it or to start interfering.'

Emma flung her a look of amusement. 'Isn't there just a chance you're making a somewhat personal judgement here? I've heard he's a damn good doctor, and obviously he has plans...'

'Hah! I'll bet.'

Emma frowned. 'Look, I know how strongly you feel about your rheumatology research, and how hard you've worked, but...well, has he actually *said* he intends to interfere in your work or to change anything?'

'No, not yet. But give it time.'

'Has it occurred to you that maybe he's just interested in *you*?' Emma gave her a mischievous, sidelong glance. 'Perhaps you made more of an impression than you thought.'

Beth stirred her coffee with unnecessary briskness. She had asked herself that same question, and the conclusions she had come to were so completely illogical that she had discarded them almost as quickly as they had arisen.

The only thing likely to make any impression on Dr D'Angelo's thick hide would be a ten-ton rhino at full gallop! And even then came the suspicion that he would deal with it without as much of a flicker of the dark eyelashes.

She put her cup down decisively. 'Shall we drop the subject and get back to work? It would be nice to get off duty on time for once.'

One look at her friend's face persuaded Emma to let the matter drop, though not without a deep sense of regret for what she considered to be a terrible waste of a life.

She had known Paul Bryant as long as she had known Beth, and she hadn't liked what she had known, but had wisely kept her own counsel. She had watched their romance grow, had been a bridesmaid at their wedding. And it had been no consolation to discover that, even within the first weeks, the vague fears she had felt had already started to be proved correct.

She hadn't known the circumstances, and Beth had never talked about it, but she had seen her friend change from a lively, outgoing person to someone quiet and withdrawn. And yet, for some reason even she couldn't fathom, Paul's sudden and tragic death had only seemed to trap Beth in a cage of guilt from which she seemed incapable—or unwilling—to break free.

Emma set her cup down, glanced at her watch and rose to her feet, smoothing down her white dress. 'I'd better go. We've got a new student nurse, and I'm showing her the ropes.' Her smiling brown eyes hid her real concern as she waved and left the staffroom.

For the rest of the day, Beth forced herself to concentrate with such intensity on her work that, by the time she finally reached for her jacket and bag, her neck muscles were stiff with tension.

Going through to Reception, she dropped a bundle of letters on the desk. 'These are all signed, Maria. By the way, can you remind me to contact Mr Cunningham's insurance representative again tomorrow? Mr Cunningham is the gentleman who broke his leg rather badly.'

'Ah, *si*.'

'Not a very good end to his holiday, was it? Anyway, I gather she's managed to arrange a flight home for him and his family. I just need to know what the arrangements are so that I can contact the British hospital and let them know when he'll be arriving.'

'*Si, Dottore.*'

'Thanks, Maria.'

'*Prego*. You're welcome.'

'Right. In that case, I'm going home.' She smiled. '*Sono stanco*. I'm tired. I think I must have a migraine coming on.'

Maria was already rising from her seat behind the desk. 'You do look very pale. Can I get you anything? Some tablets?'

Beth shook her head, then wished she hadn't as the wave of pain increased until it was like a tight band round her skull. 'No, *grazie*, Maria. I have some medication at home. I'll take some as soon as I get in, and have an early night.'

She looked at her watch and had difficulty focusing on its tiny face. 'I'll see you tomorrow, then.'

Climbing into her car and driving home through the noisy traffic and the relentless heat, Beth nursed a growing suspicion that, if present signs were anything to go by, this was one migraine she wasn't going to be able to sleep off.

The apartment at least was cool and welcoming. Her actions purely automatic, she kicked off her shoes and padded across the tiled floor to open shutters, letting in a welcome breeze before going to run a bath.

Having made coffee, she swallowed two of the strong painkillers prescribed by her doctor. She knew that, ideally, she should have taken them at the very first signs of the migraine, but it had been so long since she had last suffered one of the debilitating headaches that, she realised now, she had become complacent and had left the tablets at home. Still, better late than never.

Going into the bedroom, she stripped off her clothes and stood naked in front of the mirror as she slipped her arms into the sleeves of a silk kimono. Without any sense of false modesty, she knew that she had a good figure. Admittedly she had lost weight in the past four years, but the honing of a little excess flesh was all to the good.

The shock came when she stared at features scarcely recognisable as her own. Her eyes were like huge green smudges in her pale face, and she turned away quickly as hot tears began to well up. Yet the strange thing was that she didn't even know why she was crying, or for whom. She hadn't even wept when Paul had been killed. They had said it was delayed shock, but surely four years was too long?

Dashing away the tears, Beth made for the bathroom. She had shed her robe and was about to step into the steaming, perfumed water when the doorbell rang. Groaning inwardly, she told herself she would ignore it. Whoever it was would soon give up and go away.

Sighing, she eased herself into the scented bubbles

and lay back, closing her eyes to block out the pain which was tightening round her forehead.

The doorbell rang again, longer and more insistently this time, as if the caller was becoming angry. Beth's fist slammed with annoyance against the bath as she dragged herself out of the water again and shrugged the silk robe over her wet body. Whoever it was had better have a good reason...

'*Lascuami in pace*,' she muttered under her breath. 'Leave me in peace.' She wrenched the door open and felt the colour flood into her cheeks as she stared in disbelief at the figure standing there.

'You!' For several seconds, shock held her rigid as Nick D'Angelo's gaze swept with slow appreciation over her body, the dark eyes taking in every curve, every outline which, she realised, blushing hotly, must be visible beneath the damp robe. Involuntarily, she pulled it more securely around her in a jerky movement, her flush deepening as his mouth curved with silent amusement.

He smiled. 'Good evening.'

She felt oddly flustered. 'Er... Good evening. What are you doing here?'

'I'm sorry if this is a bad time. I have tried to call you but it seems you were always busy. I was beginning to think you were avoiding me, but then I told myself, No. Why should that be? Ah, but I am forgetting. These are for you.' He produced a large bunch of flowers from behind his back.

Beth stared at them as he thrust them into her hands. 'F-for me?'

'*Si*. We didn't exactly get off to the best of starts. I think we should try again. Perhaps you should put them in water?' he suggested lightly as her nerveless fingers plucked a petal, letting it fall to the floor.

She swallowed hard. 'Water. Yes. Er... Look, I'd invite you in but—'

'That would be nice.'

He followed her into the small apartment, to the kitchen where she put the flowers on to the table and said hesitantly, 'I'd offer you a drink but—'

'Coffee would be good.'

She sighed, flipped the switch on the electric kettle and reached for coffee and mugs as he leaned nonchalantly against the work surface. She spooned sugar into her own coffee and handed him a mug before leading the way into the sitting room.

'You still haven't explained why you're here. I've had a long day, Dr—'

'Nick. We agreed.'

She sighed. 'Nick. I have a splitting headache, so perhaps you can tell me what it is that you want.'

'I thought we should talk. You didn't answer my calls.'

'I was busy. You surely don't expect me to leave a patient in order to chat.' His close proximity was having a strangely disturbing effect on her nerves. 'You could have left a message with Maria.'

'I don't deal with secretaries.' He sipped at his coffee and looked at her. 'As a matter of interest, would you have returned my calls anyway?'

Her head was throbbing, and as her fingers probed the spot she was surprised to discover that her hands were actually shaking. 'Would there have been much point? I'm sure you've already made your plans and nothing I could say would change them. I think we said all there was to say and I think we both know where we stand.'

His brown eyes regarded her with an unreadable expression. 'I'm sorry you're not happy about me joining the team.'

'I didn't say that.'

'You didn't have to. You have a remarkably expressive face. The question that intrigues me is why?'

'Why?' She cleared her throat.

'Oh, I know about Max leaving. I can understand why you should feel sad. But I sense there is more to it. Is it something I've inadvertently done—or said?'

'I really don't know what you mean.' She turned and as she did so her body brushed against his, sending a mass of ill-timed signals running through her. Startled, she glanced up at him and drew herself up sharply. 'Why should you think that?'

'I've no idea. Suppose you tell me.'

Her chin lifted. 'It isn't personal.'

'I'd like to believe that. I'm not looking for a fight, Beth. I'm not the enemy, I'm just here to do a job. I'd like to feel I was welcome.'

'Maybe that's it.' She looked at him sharply. 'No one really knows why you're here—what your plans are. Can you blame people for being wary?'

A spasm flickered across his face. 'Maybe not. But I can give you my word, I do have the best interests of the hospital at heart. I did come here to talk business.'

'You could have used the telephone.'

'I tried—remember? You were being particularly evasive.'

'So, what exactly was so important that it couldn't wait?'

'I had a meeting with the sponsors.'

'I see. And you couldn't wait to bring the bad news, is that it? So, when does it happen? When do they close us down?'

'What makes you think that's what they want to do?'

She threw him a scathing glance. 'The alternative would be to spend money—a lot of it. To update equipment, to renovate…'

'I agree, and, as it happens, so do they.'

'They—they do?'

His mouth curved with laughter. 'You've made up your mind that I'm the villain of the piece, haven't you? Well, I'm sorry to disappoint you but I happen to agree. The hospital fulfils a need. We have a large and still growing expatriate community in the area, and I'd like to see us handling more non-paying cases. So, far from closing down, I can see that it makes sense to improve, to expand the service we offer.'

'Really?'

'You know your trouble, Beth? You've allowed yourself to become cynical.' He took an envelope from his inner jacket pocket and handed it to her. 'This is the reason I came. In spite of what you may think, I do have your interests at heart. I think you should read that report. It outlines some of the ideas the sponsors and I shared. I'm sure you'll find it interesting, and I'm sure you'll have your own ideas. If you can come up with facts and figures to back them up, we can discuss them over lunch tomorrow. I'll pick you up at one o'clock.'

'I'm on duty, and I don't do lunch.'

'Make an exception.' He smiled. 'This is Italy. Everyone does lunch. Besides, as I said, it is in your interests. By the way, when do you take your next clinic?'

'Clinic?'

'Still's disease—juvenile arthritis. You did say you were carrying out a research programme.'

'Well, yes. As a matter of fact, it's tomorrow, at ten-thirty.'

'Fine. I'll join you.'

'But…' She stared at him. 'Why?'

'Because I'm interested. I want to see you work. What your aims are, where it's all leading.'

'In other words, I have to justify my work.'

'We all have to do that, Beth,' he said softly. 'Is it so unreasonable? If the project is to continue, you'll need funding. I need to convince the sponsors, therefore *I* must be convinced. So, I'll see you at ten-thirty. We can have lunch afterwards. At the café in the square.'

'I'm on a diet,' she insisted firmly.

'You don't need to diet. It's lunch, Beth. That's all.' He put his empty coffee-mug down. 'It's getting late. I should go.'

She turned to find his face suddenly very close to her own. She stood stock still, held, almost as if by accident, in the warm circle of his arm. His skin smelled faintly of aftershave and she was totally unprepared for the way in which, for those few seconds, she seemed to respond to that brief contact.

Her breath snagged in her throat as she became aware of his frowning gaze, of the sensual mouth just a breath away, so close that her nostrils were invaded by the clean, musky smell of him.

She closed her eyes as his thumb brushed briefly against her cheek, sending a riot of sensations running through her. He smelt of aftershave and danger, though she couldn't for the life of her have explained why.

Then the phone rang. She drew a deep breath, shivering slightly as he released her. 'I have to answer that. It might be important. Can...can you see yourself out?'

His mouth made a crooked shape. 'Saved by the bell, Beth?'

She ignored him and moved towards the phone, surprised to find that her hand was actually shaking as she lifted the receiver.

'Yes? Dr Bryant speaking.'

'Hello, Beth. It's James. I haven't called at a bad time, have I?'

'James! No, no, of course you haven't called at a bad time.' Her face lit with pleasure.

'You sound a little tense, darling. You're sure I haven't interrupted anything?'

'No, of course you're not interrupting anything.' She flicked a glance at Nick, and couldn't suppress a hint of mischief. 'As a matter of fact, you couldn't have called at a better time. I was feeling bored. I've promised myself an early night with a good book. What can I do for you?'

James sounded slightly flustered. 'Actually, I rang to ask you to have lunch with me tomorrow. I still feel a bit guilty about what happened.'

'James, why on earth should you feel guilty?

There's really no need. It was hardly your fault that the sponsors decided to pull out.'

'Even so, I think we need to talk. I'd like a chance to put the record straight. I didn't have much option, you know—about keeping things fairly hush-hush, I mean. Things were more or less taken out of my hands. This D'Angelo chap doesn't strike me as the sort to let anything or anyone stand in his way. I'd avoid him like the plague if I were you, Beth.'

She glanced at Nick, and had to suppress the uncanny feeling that he could hear every word James said.

'I'm sure you're right. Thanks for the advice.' She took a deep breath. 'Oh, and about lunch tomorrow—it's a lovely idea. Thanks for asking me. I'd like it very much. We'll have lots to talk about.'

She almost winced to hear the deliberately provocative note in her own voice, but she had no intention of allowing herself to be dictated to by Nick D'Angelo. She smiled. 'I'll see you tomorrow, then. Same place as usual. I'll look forward to it.'

She rang off, studiously avoiding the expression in Nick's eyes.

'I thought you'd left.'

'I'm on my way.' He paused at the door. 'So, I'll take that as a no, shall I?'

'I...I'm sorry.'

He gave a short laugh. 'Oh, I don't give up that easily, Doctor.' He opened the door. 'I suggest you get a good night's sleep. You're going to need it. I'll see you tomorrow.'

After he had gone she stood for a long time in the light from one solitary lamp, her figure unconsciously graceful. Suddenly she felt exhausted and was shocked when she looked at her watch to discover that it was late. Her head was still pounding, yet somehow she still felt reluctant to go to bed, until common sense told her that she had to get up and go to work again in a few hours.

For some totally illogical reason her pulse rate was still racing. Beth drew in a sharp breath. For the first time in a long while a sudden feeling of loneliness swept through her, threatening to overwhelm her in its intensity. Damn him! Damn Nick D'Angelo!

Removing her robe, Beth slid naked between the sheets and closed her eyes, but it was still a long time before she slept. She tossed and turned for what seemed an eternity before falling asleep just before dawn, only to discover that in her dreams she wasn't as safe as in reality, and when she was woken, gasping with shock, to the sound of the telephone ringing, her body was filmed with sweat.

She fought her way out of the sheet, groaning as she struggled to rid her drugged brain of the last remnants of sleep. She hadn't imagined it—the phone *was* ringing. Her gaze flew to the clock, certain she must have overslept, only to groan with disbelief as she saw that it read seven o'clock. Brushing her mane of hair back, she reached for the phone and lay back against the pillow, the receiver pressed against her ear.

'Yes?' Her voice came out thick and heavy with sleep, and there was a momentary pause before the voice at the other end replied.

'I'm sorry. Did I wake you?'

If she hadn't been fully awake before, she certainly was now as she sat up, hot colour flushing her cheeks.

'Nick. Wh—? No.' She gritted her teeth firmly on the lie. 'Of course you didn't wake me. I've been awake for ages. I was just making coffee as a matter of fact.'

She thought she heard him laugh and she sat up now, fully awake, and groped for the sheet, only to remind herself crossly that she was being ridiculous. He couldn't possibly know that she was naked.

'Beth, are you still there?' There was a faint hint of concern in his voice.

'What? Oh, yes, of course I'm still here.' She raked a hand through her hair. 'Have you any idea what time it is, Doctor? I take it you have a very good reason for calling me so early?'

'It was Nick a moment ago, before you had time to remember to put the barriers up.'

She swallowed hard. It seemed that even from a distance he had the power to disturb her senses. 'I was busy,' she said briskly. 'You took me by surprise. So, what exactly was it that you wanted? I do have to get ready and go to work. I have a particularly busy day ahead.'

'And a lunch date, of course. Let's not forget that.'

'Of course.' Her voice held a deliberate challenge, and she sensed he was suddenly angry.

There was a momentary pause again, and this time she was the one to break it. 'Nick, are you still there?'

'Yes, I'm still here. And you're right, I have a busy day, too. Which is why I called so early. I appreciate that you can't make lunch, so I'll pick you up this evening for dinner—shall we say seven-thirty?'

Beth gave a short laugh. 'But I don't... We don't have a date.'

'You're right,' he said evenly. 'We don't. What I'm suggesting is strictly a business meeting. There are things we need to discuss, things which cannot be avoided, however much you might wish it. This won't just go away, Beth. *I* won't go away. Perhaps we'll talk better on neutral ground. So, I'll pick you up later, then. Say seven-thirty? I've booked a table.'

She felt her heart give an illogical extra thud. 'Make it eight.' She slammed down the phone, but not before she was sure she had heard him laugh quietly.

CHAPTER THREE

THE air was still pleasantly cool as Beth drove to the hospital. Later the heat would build, and sensible Italians would close their shops, leave their businesses and make their way to one of the many cafés and bars to join friends and enjoy a leisurely lunch, sitting in the shade of a colourful awning.

It was one of the things she loved about this country, Beth thought. The pace of life was governed by the sun—people laughed more, families gathered together to eat and play. Italy had begun to weave its own special kind of spell from the moment she had arrived here, and she knew that it had become all too easy to fall beneath it.

She drew herself up sharply. Maybe it was a mistake to think this way. She shouldn't have let herself become too attached to it. What if things became so impossible that she couldn't go on working here?

But then the thought intruded, What future was there for her in England now? How could she go back and just pick up the pieces as if nothing had happened? On the other hand, if she stayed it meant she would have to work with Nick, and for some reason that thought was equally disturbing.

She started as, almost as if her thoughts had conjured him up, Nick appeared suddenly at her side as she carefully parked her car in the shade and locked the door.

'Good morning.' He fell smoothly into step beside her as she headed for Reception.

'Good morning *again*,' she said, pointedly.

'Coffee?'

She drew a deep, controlling breath and shook her head. 'No. Thank you, but I really do have a very busy day ahead.'

'And you'd rather I wasn't part of it.' He smiled. 'Sorry, Beth, I can't oblige. Besides, I'm intrigued. Juvenile arthritis isn't something I know a great deal about.'

'Not many people do, unless it happens to affect them or their family personally.' She juggled her briefcase and a pile of buff folders, walking ahead of him through the automatic doors towards the desk. 'Good morning, Maria.'

'Buongiorno, Dottore.' The girl transferred her smile to Nick. 'Ah, and Dottore D'Angelo.'

'Maria.' He smiled, showing even, white teeth. 'How is your papa? I hear he is not so well. A chill, is it?'

'Oh, he is much better, thank you, *Dottore*. Mamma fusses over him.' She laughed. 'Papa doesn't like to be fussed over. She says he should eat more and drink less wine. Papa says the pasta is the food of the gods, but a man can only eat so much, and a glass or two of wine never did his papa any harm since he was ninety-two when he died.'

'Well, you can't argue with that.'

Maria laughed. Beth looked from one to the other and said peevishly, 'Excuse me, I hate to break this up, but some of us have work to do. Do you have my appointments diary, Maria?'

'*Si, Dottore.* Oh, and there are a couple of messages.' She handed over a piece of paper.

'Morning, Beth.' Maggie Thomas smiled as she walked into Reception. 'And Dr D'Angelo. How are you this morning?'

Beth sighed. 'We've been through all that. Can we possibly make a start? I have a lot to get through.'

'And a lunch date, of course,' Nick murmured softly.

She threw him a look. 'And, as you say, a lunch date.' Her voice threw out a deliberate challenge and she sensed he was suddenly angry.

'*Bene.* Shall we proceed, then?'

She stifled a feeling of exasperation as he strode away, leaving her to follow.

'Oh, Beth, you'll need this as well.' Maggie handed her another file.

'Why? What is it?'

'Young Suzie Barzini's notes.'

'Suzie?' Beth frowned. 'I didn't think I was due to see her in the rheumatology clinic for another month.'

'No, you weren't, but her mother is worried. Suzie's symptoms have flared up again. I gather she's in quite a lot of pain, so I said I was sure you'd make time to see her.'

'Yes, of course.' In the treatment room, Beth shrugged off her short-sleeved jacket and hung it over the back of her chair. A quick glance in the mirror showed her reflection, neat in the denim skirt and pastel-coloured T-shirt. It also showed her Nick, seated comfortably in a chair, looking far too relaxed as he watched her.

Flushing slightly, she moved to sit at her desk. 'Er, would you—?'

'Not at all.' He waved a hand. 'You carry on. Just pretend I'm not here.'

If only that were possible! She pushed the thought away as Maggie ushered in her first patient.

'Suzie. Come in and sit down. Hello, Mrs Barzini. How are you both?'

'I am fine, Doctor. It's young Suzie who's not so well. I know her next appointment is not due for a while...'

'Please, don't worry about it. You know I'm happy to see Suzie any time.' Beth smiled. She had come to know Kate Barzini quite well over the past two years. Married to an Italian she had met in England, they had moved to live in Italy in the hope that the warmer climate might help their daughter's painful medical condition. 'By the way, this is my colleague, Dr D'Angelo. He'll be sitting in on this session, if that's all right with you?'

Mrs Barzini nodded, smiling shyly at Nick.

Beth quickly scanned the notes on her computer screen and turned to smile at the child. 'Hello, Suzie. Mum says you're not feeling too well?'

'No, not really.' The blonde-haired twelve-year-old looked at her mother, then at Beth. Suzie had first been referred to a specialist at the age of six after complaining of persistent pain in her legs and generally feeling unwell. Examination at the time had showed that both knees were affected by arthritis.

'How old are you now, Suzie? Eleven...?'

'Twelve.'

'Right, and how are the knees?'

'Hot and swollen, and they hurt when I walk.' Suzie hitched up her skirt, allowing Beth to gently examine the affected joints.

'Hmm, yes, I can see. They're both quite badly swollen, aren't they? Is the pain worse than before?'

The girl nodded, and bit at her lower lip nervously.

Nick had quietly risen to his feet and moved forward to smile at the girl and her mother. 'Hello, there.' He knelt beside Suzie, watching her reaction sympathetically as Beth made as gentle an examination as possible. He frowned. 'Do any other joints hurt, or is it just the knees?'

Beth smiled at the girl. 'At the last clinic you said that your fingers and wrists were painful, too. That's right, isn't it, Suzie?'

Nick said quietly, 'Can I take a look?'

Beth looked at him. 'As long as Suzie doesn't mind.'

He smiled. 'Is that all right, Suzie? I just want to take a quick look. I promise I'll try not to hurt you.'

Beth watched as he made his examination, his strong hands moving with surprising gentleness as he flexed the girl's hands. 'Yes, I can see they're still quite hot and swollen. And is it like this all the time, or is it worse in the mornings?'

'In the mornings.'

He glanced at Beth. 'Is that unusual?'

'No, as a matter of fact, it's fairly typical of this type of arthritis.'

'It must make things like washing and getting dressed quite difficult.' He spoke softly to Suzie.

'She's used to it now, aren't you, love?' Kate

smoothed her daughter's hair. 'Things take a bit longer, but you get there, don't you, pet?'

Suzie nodded and said shyly, 'It's a nuisance, though.'

'I'm sure it is.' Nick straightened up and looked at Beth. 'I take it Suzie's condition has been pretty well controlled by medication until now?'

'That's right.'

'So what would cause the condition to flare up suddenly?'

'It could be due to a number of things. A change in medication—which doesn't apply in Suzie's case. Until now she's been doing quite well on the dosage prescribed. The trick with any patient suffering from arthritis or rheumatism is to find the right drug and the right dosage. It could be down to stress.' She looked at Suzie. 'Have you been worried about anything in particular lately? Exams at school, perhaps? Anything like that?'

'No.'

'She has been a bit off colour this past couple of months, Doctor.' Kate Barzini said.

'Well, that could certainly explain it. What exactly was the problem?'

'Suzie had a sore throat that didn't seem to clear, and she was just...well, generally out of sorts.'

'She did see a doctor about her symptoms?'

'Oh, yes. He thought it was a viral throat infection.'

'That could certainly account for the flare-up.'

Nick frowned. 'Is it a problem? I mean, won't it just clear up, given time?'

'Well, it can, but a flare-up can reduce a patient's appetite, which might, in turn, cause anaemia. Obviously we need to get things back on an even keel again. You're still taking your usual medication—the anti-inflammatory tablets?'

Suzie nodded. 'I always take them with food, like you said to, so that they don't give me indigestion.'

'And you take painkillers if the pain is particularly bad?' Beth glanced at her computer screen again. 'I'll try you on a short course of corticosteroids, just for a few days, to reduce the swelling and inflammation.'

'I'd like that. It's a bit of a nuisance at school when I can't play with my friends because they can run faster than I can.'

'I'm sure it must be.' Beth smiled sympathetically. 'So, we can either do this through tablets or an injection into the joints. You've had them before, haven't you?'

Suzie pulled a face. 'I'd rather have the tablets.'

'I can't say I blame you,' Beth replied. 'OK, we'll try you on a course of steroid anti-inflammatory tablets for a short period.' She tapped out the prescription. 'Obviously we don't want to keep you on them for longer than is absolutely necessary, but in the short term they should, hopefully, reduce the inflammation.' She handed the prescription to Kate. 'See how it goes. If things haven't improved in a week, bring Suzie to see me again and we'll have a rethink, but I'm pretty sure these tablets will do the trick.'

She saw them both out and returned to her desk to find Nick peering at her notes. He glanced up, frowning. 'You must find it fairly depressing, seeing young children in so much pain. How do you deal with it?'

He sounded genuinely concerned. She looked at him and almost wished she hadn't as she stood mesmerised by the sensations that coursed through her. Her breath caught in her throat as a new realisation came homing in on her bemused senses. If she wasn't very careful, there was every danger of her becoming seriously attracted to Nick D'Angelo, and that wouldn't do. It wouldn't do at all.

She swallowed hard. 'On the contrary, I don't find it in the least depressing. The children I meet are mostly cheerful, well adjusted and incredibly brave. I see my role as one of encouragement. Yes, I treat their pain in whatever way seems appropriate, but I also try to show them that, in spite of the limitations arthritis places on their lives, they can still lead active, useful lives.'

'Even so, it can't be easy.'

'No, not always.' She gave a slight laugh as she tidied her desk. 'But I think I have the easiest part. When a child has arthritis, and some are much younger than Suzie, it doesn't affect just one person—it can affect the whole family. Suzie is a fairly typical case, but there are different kinds of arthritis. It can affect all age groups. The complications can vary—symptoms can vary.'

He was half sitting on the desk, hands in pockets. 'You've obviously become quite an expert.'

'No, I'm far from that. I'm still learning. I think I told you that I became interested for personal reasons. I took rheumatology as my specialty subject in medical school.'

'I imagine it was useful in general practice.'

'Very. And it just so happened that when I came here and people knew of my interest in the subject, patients began to be referred to me. I've learned a lot as I've gone along. My research project has helped.'

'And how many patients do you see in a typical session?'

'I don't know that there is a typical session. Yes, I see regular patients but, as in Suzie's case, there are often emergencies.' She looked at him sharply. 'Why the interest? Or is this a precursor to saying that the numbers don't justify the expense and time? Is that all that this is about? A cost-cutting exercise? I wonder why I'm not surprised.'

His gaze narrowed as he straightened up and glanced at his watch. 'I can't stop you drawing conclusions, founded or unfounded. As I said, we do need to talk but obviously this isn't the time or the place, which is why I booked a table at Antonio's.' He frowned as if he sensed she was about to protest. 'I meant what I said, Doctor. This is strictly business. I'd like to know more about your research and how it helps people like Suzie, but this isn't the only department. I have to consider the needs of the hospital as a whole and I have ideas of my own. I take it you did read the report I left with you?'

'Yes.' She frowned. 'Well, most of it. It was fairly lengthy.'

'Then I'd say we have a lot to discuss. Things *are* going to change, Beth. We can work together or, if necessary, I'll do it without you, but it will happen. You must at least have formed an opinion, some ideas as to how we can make beneficial changes?'

She frowned. 'Why would you value my opinion? You'll do whatever it is you've decided to do.'

'That isn't true,' he said evenly. 'You know the

way things work around here. You must have worked out the bad points as well as the good. As a senior member of staff your input is important. Or maybe you don't think you'd fit in as part of a new, highly motivated team?'

'No!' The protest came sharply. 'I'm saying that Max was a good doctor and a good friend. He worked damned hard to make this hospital what it is.'

'I don't deny it, but Max isn't here any more. Times change. The demands on the medical services have grown. Max would be the first to admit that. Or maybe you're afraid of change.'

'No!'

'So what have you got to lose?'

Quite a lot, she thought ruefully, as if he didn't know. Not least a job she loved, a way of life.

Into the silence, he said, 'I'm asking you to work with me, Beth. Can you afford to turn this opportunity down?'

'What do you mean?'

'You're a doctor.'

'There are other doctors.'

'True. But don't tell me your loyalties don't lie here, Beth, because I won't believe it. And in any case, where would you go from here?' he said softly. 'Back to England, to whatever it is you ran away from? Is that really what you want?'

Colour darkened her cheeks and she was still thinking of a response when someone tapped at the door and Maggie popped her head round. She looked anxious.

'Oh, Beth, I'm sorry to interrupt, but we have an

emergency admission on the way. They should be here in a couple of minutes. Can you come?'

Beth was already reaching for her stethoscope and heading for the door. 'Do we have any details?'

'Not a lot, but it's Mrs Craig.'

'Alice!' Beth felt her heart give a sudden jolt.

'I know you know her quite well. I thought you'd want to know.'

'Yes. Thanks, I appreciate it. I'm on my way.' At the door she hesitated and flung a glance at Nick. 'Look, I'm sorry—'

'Don't be,' he said briskly. 'I'm coming with you.'

He was beside her as they hurried along the corridor towards the emergency room. 'I take it she's a friend of yours?'

'I've known Alice and her husband for a couple of years. They bought a small retirement place out here, quite close to the hospital.' A swing door responded to the pressure of her hand as she hurried through. 'I met them when Ted started coming to my clinic. He's had arthritis for years. They're a lovely couple.'

'She's in here.' Maggie held the door of the small waiting room open and Ted Craig greeted their arrival with obvious relief.

'Oh, Doctor, thank you for coming so quickly. I know how busy you are.'

'It's no bother, Ted,' Beth reassured him gently. 'It's what I'm here for. It's Alice, isn't it?'

He blew his nose and dabbed at his eyes with a large hanky. 'They've taken her into that cubicle there.' He walked with difficulty, supported by a walking stick as he led them to where his wife lay on an examination couch. 'I don't know what's the matter with her, Doctor. She got up early this morning as usual. You know Alice. She's never been one for taking things easy, even though we're retired.'

'I do indeed, Ted. This is Dr D'Angelo, by the way. My colleague.'

Nick smiled. 'Can you tell us what happened, Ted?'

'Well, she didn't seem too bad. A bit slower than usual but, then, at our age there's no reason to rush, is there? She said her chest felt a bit tight, that was all. She'd been doing a bit of gardening, thought she might have overdone it a bit. We didn't think too much about it.'

Nick glanced at Beth who said quietly, 'Has she actually complained of any pain, Ted?'

'That's why I called the ambulance. She didn't want me to, but I could see she wasn't right.' Leaning heavily on his stick, Ted pushed open the door. 'She's in here. They've made her as comfortable as they can.'

'When did the pain start?' Nick asked gently.

'About an hour ago—maybe a bit more. I think she felt it a bit earlier but didn't say anything. I knew something was wrong but she wouldn't let me call anyone. Stubborn old thing.' His eyes misted with tears.

Nick quickly rested a hand on the man's shoulder. 'Don't worry, Ted. Dr Bryant and I are going to do everything we possibly can to make her better.'

Beth moved close to the examination couch where seventy-year-old Alice Craig lay huddled beneath a sheet. She was pale and clearly in severe pain. Beads of sweat had gathered on her forehead but she was still conscious.

She moved her head restlessly against the pillows and tried to speak, but it was clearly an effort for her to get her breath.

Nick said quickly, 'Don't try to talk, Alice. Just relax. Can you show us where the pain is?'

One frail hand went shakily to the centre of her chest and moved slowly in the direction of her left arm. 'Here… Heavy.'

'All right, Alice. You try to relax now. We're going to give you something to ease the pain and to help you breathe more easily.' Beth's fingers automatically reached for the pulse in the woman's neck. She glanced at Nick and he produced his stethoscope, making a gentle but thorough examination. After a few minutes he straightened up.

'What is it, Doctor? What's wrong with her?'

Nick looked into Ted's watery eyes. 'I'm afraid it looks as if Alice has had a heart attack, Ted. But I think it's only a mild one. I know that may not be much consolation right now, but we're going to deal with it. The important thing now is to get her some pain relief and to try to make her feel more comfortable.'

The old man reached out shakily to grasp Beth's hand. She held onto it firmly and looked at him, seeing the fear in his eyes.

'We'll look after her, Ted. She's in the best place and she'll get the best of care, I promise.'

'I want to stay with her.'

'Yes, of course you do. We'll arrange that for you.' She glanced at Maggie, who nodded. 'We'll deal with the paperwork and get her admitted. In the meantime, why don't you sit with Alice—hold her hand? I'm sure she'd like that.'

She glanced at Nick and he nodded imperceptibly towards the door. 'You're not happy about her, are you?'

'Alice is not exactly robust at the best of times.' She looked up at him. 'She'll probably be hospitalised for some time, depending on her progress, of course. I'm not sure how Ted is going to cope without her.'

'Well, let's hope he won't have to. Look, I'll get her started on something to ease the pain. Do you know if they have any relatives?'

'I'm pretty sure there's a daughter back in England, but I'm not sure where. I'll talk to Ted and see if I can persuade him to let me give her a call. Right now I think they need all the support they can get.'

'I agree. In the meantime, would you like me to get the ECG and the blood studies started?'

'Oh, would you? I'd appreciate it. By the way...' Turning, she almost collided with his solid, muscular frame. For several seconds he stared down at her, the sensual mouth only inches from her own. She found herself holding her breath as a strange new sense of awareness brought the faint colour to her cheeks. 'I...er... Thanks for your help. I'm grateful.'

Nick drew himself up, frowning. 'Forget it. Like I said, Beth, I'm not the enemy. I'm a doctor. It's what I'm here for.'

She looked at him, seeing the generous, mobile curve of his mouth, the faint lines around his eyes, and she felt a strange compulsion to reach up and touch his face with her fingertips.

Instead, she drew herself up and said breathlessly, 'Yes, well…' She glanced at her watch. 'I'd better go and talk to Ted and try to reassure Alice.'

'You're right.' His mouth tightened fractionally and briefly she wondered why. 'And, of course, you don't want to be late for your lunch with James, do you?'

CHAPTER FOUR

JAMES was sitting at a table beneath a colourful sun awning. The café was already thronged with customers as Beth hurried across the piazza towards him, a smile on her lips, an attractive figure in the cool, pale mint sleeveless dress she'd changed into, which gave quite stunning emphasis to her eyes.

'Hi,' she said breathlessly. 'Sorry I'm a bit late.'

'Not to worry.' James had already ordered drinks. His own glass was empty, her glass of orange juice stood waiting. James knew her tastes and didn't need to ask what she wanted. He half rose to his feet to kiss her cheek as he made way for her at the table. 'I got here a bit early. Just as well I did. The place is bursting at the seams.'

'It always is. Luigi's is popular.'

'I was afraid you weren't going to make it.'

Beth settled into the seat and drew a breath of relief. The afternoon heat was almost stifling. 'I was beginning to wonder myself. The clinic seemed to take longer than usual, then we had an emergency admission. It was Alice Craig. Ted Craig's wife. Do you remember them? I'm sure I introduced you.'

'I can't say I do offhand. But, then, I see so many patients.' James smiled indulgently. 'I've told you before, my darling, you're far too conscientious. Couldn't someone else have dealt with it?'

'No, I don't think so.' She frowned. 'Not really.

Alice has had a heart attack. She knows me and I thought it might reassure her to see someone she knows. Look, I am sorry,' she reiterated. 'I did try to phone you but you'd already left the clinic.'

Sensing a vague peevishness in James, she forced herself to smile. 'Anyway, let's not talk about work. I've been looking forward to this.' She looked around the noisy café. 'I missed our lunchtime chats while I was on leave.'

James seemed satisfied. 'That's OK.' He proffered the menu. 'I know how it is. I just think you need to be a little tougher sometimes, that's all, my sweet. Still, you made it, that's what counts, especially under the circumstances. Perhaps we'd better order, or we shan't get any lunch.' He shot her a curious look and Beth frowned, puzzled by his words. What could he possibly mean…under the circumstances? What circumstances?

She batted the thought away as James looked rather pointedly at his watch, and said sheepishly, 'I have to be back in an hour. You know how it is. Everyone's afraid of upsetting the new boss.'

Beth smiled. 'Since when did you worry about that?'

'Yes, well…' James pulled a face. 'Can't be too careful, can we? I mean, new broom and all that. Besides, we're pretty busy. You know what it's like this time of year. Tourists arriving in droves. Not that I'm complaining,' he said quickly, almost too quickly.

Beth looked at him over the rim of her glass and frowned. 'Poor James. Things can't be easy for you at the moment, I realise that. I mean, well, you haven't talked about it much, but I know you always hoped that when Max retired you would be offered the medical director's job.'

'It would have been nice.' There was an edge to James's voice. 'By rights I *was* in line for it. Max had always spoken as if it would happen.' He tapped his fingers impatiently on the table. 'Still, I suppose I should be grateful I've got a job at all—the way things are going. I suppose you've heard the rumours that he wants to hold extra clinics for non-paying patients? Heaven knows, the staff are already working at full stretch, and if there are redundancies…'

'We don't know that yet, do we? Not for sure. I mean…well, don't you think we should at least give Nick a chance?'

'Nick?' James's mouth twisted. 'I hadn't realised you were already on first-name terms. It didn't take long, did it?'

As James looked at her Beth took refuge in studying the menu, feeling strangely relieved as the waiter arrived to take their order.

She chose a salad as a compromise between her lack of appetite and not wanting to offend James, and when it came she ate with relish, surprised to discover that she was quite hungry after all. James tucked into a pizza and, when they had finished, ordered coffees.

Beth stirred sugar into hers and sat back with a sigh of satisfaction. 'Mmm. That was nice, but definitely naughty. I keep promising myself I'll skip lunch. It plays havoc with the diet.'

'You don't need to diet.' James's gaze studied the slender curves of her figure in a way Beth found strangely comforting. And yet she sensed a hint of reserve now, which puzzled her until she thought she guessed the reason. She leaned forward, resting her arms on the table.

'James, you're not blaming yourself for what's happened, are you? Because, if so, there's really no need. We all knew that Max was thinking about retiring some time in the not too distant future, but no one could possibly have foreseen that he would leave so suddenly. No one blames you. *I* don't hold you responsible, you do know that?'

For a moment he looked startled, then an uncomfortable flush coloured his cheeks. 'I couldn't exactly blame you if you did, though I swear my hands were tied. While you were on leave I heard a whisper that something was going on, that the sponsors were planning to bring in a sharpshooter to replace Max. I wanted to warn you, but I was told that the whole thing was confidential and anyone breaking that confidentiality would suffer the consequences.' His hand ran through his hair. 'Hell, Beth, I was as stunned as everyone else by what actually happened—by how quickly it happened.'

'It would have been nice to have had some warning but, of course, I understand that you couldn't say anything before an announcement was made. I expect I'd have done exactly the same thing.'

James still seemed uneasy. 'I just thought...' He dropped his gaze to his empty coffee-cup. 'Well, I thought you might feel I'd been a bit disloyal—to you, that is.'

Beth frowned, unable to help him with whatever battle it was he was fighting. She gave a small sigh, impatient that he wouldn't let the matter drop. 'James, what is it you're trying to say?'

His mouth tightened. 'Well, I suppose I'd rather imagined…hoped that we had a pretty strong relationship.' His eyes rose to look at her directly, and for some reason she sensed that he was angry. 'At least, that was what I thought. It seems I was mistaken, in which case I'm sorry. I just wish I'd known, that's all.'

Beth stared at him, her mouth slightly open on a protest against something she didn't even begin to understand. 'James, I have no idea what you're talking about. We're friends, or at least I thought we were. Very good friends.'

He gave a short laugh. 'I'm grateful, but I'd rather hoped we were something more than just good friends. I guess I've been pretty naïve, in more ways than one. I thought you were off men in general. I hadn't figured it was just me. You should have told me how things were between you and D'Angelo. I'd have backed off.' His laugh had an edge to it. 'I do realise I don't stand a chance against that sort of competition. I'm just surprised, that's all. I mean, judging from the way things were when the two of you met…' He frowned, tapping his fingers against his cup. 'Obviously things must have taken a definite turn for the better. He must have used some pretty powerful persuasion. But, then, I've heard he's a bit of a sweet-talker.'

Beth was suddenly shaking with anger as well as shock. Fumbling clumsily for her bag, she slid out of her seat and without a backward glance began to walk across the piazza. She pushed her way through the crowds, hardly caring whether James followed her or not.

He caught up with her by the fountain. 'Beth, wait. Look, I'm sorry if I've upset you. I didn't mean—'

'Upset me?' Her mouth quivered.

'I was just shocked—surprised, that's all.' He gave her a look of pleading desperation. 'Why didn't you tell me you had someone with you when you phoned? The last thing I wanted was to cause you any embarrassment.'

'Why on earth should it have done that?'

'I would have thought it was pretty obvious.' James suddenly looked very sheepish. 'I mean... Oh, come on, Beth, if it had been anyone other than D'Angelo. Do you know what sort of reputation he's got?'

'I see.' Beth's face was ashen as understanding dawned. 'So you assume that I'm...that he and I...?' Her colour came flooding back.

James stared defensively. 'Well, you must see how it looked.'

She closed her eyes briefly, telling herself that this couldn't be happening. 'No, James. Actually, I don't know how it looked.'

'It seemed pretty obvious,' he said flatly. 'I thought when I phoned that you sounded odd. At the time I thought you were upset. Now I realise. Damn!'

He broke off abruptly and Beth looked at him, her eyes glittering dangerously. 'You realise what, James?' she said tautly.

He looked sheepish. 'Well, you sounded...flustered. I don't know, just, different, that's all. Look, I'm sorry.'

She drew a deep breath. 'There's nothing to be sorry about, James. Yes, Nick was with me when you phoned. As a matter of fact, he'd brought a report he particularly wanted me to read. It was important. But as for your assumption that there was anything more to it than that...' She met his gaze directly. 'Frankly, I really don't see that it deserves an answer.'

'Look, Beth, I'm sorry. I jumped to conclusions, but when I happened to mention to him in Reception this morning that I wanted to get away on time because I had a lunch date, he said he knew. I didn't think too much about it until he said he'd reminded you about it this morning, *before* he left for the hospital.'

She said tightly, 'That's right. He did. He telephoned me. As I would have told you, if you had asked me, James.'

He raked a hand through his hair. 'I'm concerned for you, Beth, that's all.'

'There's no reason to be,' she said sharply, and then relented slightly as she saw the misery in his face. She reached out to rest a hand on his arm. 'James, why don't you give him a chance? He's here to do a job. Things may not be as bad as you think.'

He gave a slight laugh. 'I wish I had your confidence.'

'You will have once you've worked with him, got to know him.'

'But that's the point. I don't think I can—work with him, I mean.' His mouth twisted. 'I should have been doing that job, Beth. I'm qualified.'

'Yes, I know, James, but—'

'I have a lot of ideas—good ideas.'

'I know you do. Why don't you talk to him?'

James gave an exasperated sigh. 'Because it won't

do any good. It isn't just that I can't work with the man. It's…'

'It's what, James?'

'I just thought that…that you and I…' He frowned. 'Suddenly I can see that things aren't quite as I imagined—hoped they were between us. They're not, are they, Beth? I'm worried about you.'

'There's no need.'

'I'd like to believe that. I really would.' He looked at his watch and without waiting for her to reply said, 'I have to get back. I have some paperwork to sort out. I'll give you a lift. You're on duty this afternoon, aren't you?'

She nodded. 'It's all right. I'll walk. I need some time to think.'

'Fair enough.' He turned and walked away, leaving her to stand in the middle of the crowded piazza.

Back at the hospital, she didn't see anything of Nick, which was probably just as well, she thought, as she was kept busy for the rest of the afternoon. She had just seen her last patient out and was in the office, signing letters before heading in search of a welcome cup of coffee, when she became aware of Nick coming to stand beside her at the desk. He handed a batch of case notes over to Maria.

'There you go. All finished.' He glanced at Beth, and she could almost have sworn there was a glint in his eyes. 'How was lunch?'

'Fine,' she said through gritted teeth, lowering her voice. 'No thanks to you.' A slow tide of angry colour rose in her cheeks as she rounded on him. 'How *dare* you do that to me?'

His dark brows drew together. 'Do what?'

'You know very well what,' she snarled, moving fractionally away from the desk as she became aware of Maria glancing curiously in their direction. 'How could you—?' She broke off with a sigh of exasperation as Maggie hurried towards them. The young woman gave a sigh of relief as she saw Nick.

'Oh, Dr D'Angelo, I'm glad I caught you. We've just had an emergency admission. Do you think you could take a look?'

He was instantly professional. 'What's the problem?'

'It's a small child. He seems to be in pain and is having difficulty breathing. His mother brought him in. They're on holiday, staying locally. She's obviously worried sick.'

'Yes, of course I'll come.' He frowned. 'I thought Dr Bueno was duty casualty officer?'

'Yes, he is, but a pregnant young woman came in complaining of chest pains. He's still with her.'

'In that case, I'm on my way. How old is the child?'

'Five, and he's frightened and upset.'

He swore softly under his breath as he headed for the door, then he turned to look at Beth. 'You'd better come along.'

Stifling a tiny and what she knew was a totally illogical feeling of resentment, her head jerked up. 'Is that really necessary?'

'I think so,' came the quiet response. 'I shall need to examine the child. It occurs to me that the mother is likely to be anxious. It might help if someone is on hand to offer a little moral support—don't you agree?'

'Yes, of course you're right.' She followed him, almost running in an effort to keep up. The doors leading to Casualty swung open as they entered the small emergency treatment room.

At a glance her eyes took in the child. A tearful, blond-haired five-year-old was lying on the examination couch. His eyes were closed, his breathing was rapid and uneven. His small face was flushed. His mother, looking pale and equally tearful, held her son's small hand.

Nick smiled. 'Hello. I'm Dr D'Angelo, and this is my colleague, Dr Bryant. I gather this little chap isn't feeling too well?'

'That's right. I'm so worried, Doctor. Adam seemed fine until last night—well, he'd seemed a bit tired and out of sorts during the day but, then, we're on holiday and he's been rushing around. You know what kids are like. We just thought he'd overdone things, or that he'd had a bit too much sun.' She glanced anxiously at Nick. 'He is going to be all right, isn't he?'

'We're certainly going to do everything we can to make sure he is.' He looked at Maggie. 'Do we have the notes?'

'Yes, Doctor.' She handed over a clipboard before moving to the side of the examination couch to check the child's pulse.

Nick scanned the notes and frowned slightly. Uncoiling his stethoscope from his pocket, he made a gentle but thorough examination before straightening up. 'Has Adam complained of any pain, Mrs Bates?'

'Well, he said his chest hurt. We thought perhaps

he'd had a fall, bumped himself when he was playing. You know?'

Nick nodded. 'I think it may be a little more serious than that. There's no bruising, but he is having trouble breathing.'

Beth said softly, 'How is his temperature?'

'High. Thirty-eight point nine at the last reading.' Nick handed her the notes. 'He looks flushed but he's shivering.'

'His lips look quite blue. He's certainly not very happy, is he?'

Nick moved closer to the examination couch and smiled down at the child. 'All right, Adam? My name is Dr D'Angelo, and this is Dr Bryant. We're going to make you feel better. It's not very nice, being poorly, is it?'

The child's eyes flickered open and he briefly shook his head. 'My tummy hurts.'

'Does it? Can you show me where? Just there?' Nick was a man of speedy reflexes. The reassuring smile was an added bonus. 'Right, well, suppose I take a look and see if we can do something about it?' In one calm, unhurried movement he began his examination. His hands moved to the child's chest. 'And how about there? Is that uncomfortable, too?'

Adam nodded, then coughed, a deep, loose cough that seemed to shake his small body. Beth supported him until it was over, and he lay back, exhausted, against the pillows.

Beth saw Nick frown and watched, fascinated, as his features softened and he stroked his hand gently against the child's sweat-dampened hair. 'All right, *bambino*. You take it easy. We'll leave you in peace for a while. I expect you could do with a little sleep. We'll just have a chat with your mum, then she'll come back and sit with you.'

He lowered his voice as they moved away fractionally. 'He's certainly not very well, is he?'

'What is it?' Sue Bates looked anxiously from one to the other. 'What's wrong with him, Doctor?'

Nick looked at Beth. 'I'd say pneumonia is a distinct possibility, wouldn't you?'

'Yes, I agree.'

'Oh, heavens.' Sue pressed a trembling hand to her mouth. 'That's serious, isn't it?'

Beth put an arm round the distraught woman. 'It can be,' she said softly. 'But the good thing is that you brought him to us as soon as you realised something was wrong.'

'We need to do some tests to confirm it, of course,' Nick said.

'What sort of tests?'

'We'll need to take some chest X-rays to see if there's any fluid on his lungs, and do a blood test.'

He glanced at Maggie. 'We just need to be absolutely sure what we're dealing with. Perhaps you can set things moving? I'd like the results as quickly as possible.' He smiled reassuringly at the child's mother. 'Adam will get the very best of care, I promise you. In the meantime, we need to get him settled into a bed so that we can make him more comfortable.'

Beth said gently, 'Are you and Adam holidaying alone, or do you have someone with you?'

'We...we came with my parents. They'll be worried sick. I'll have to let them know what's happening.' She fumbled in her pocket for a hanky. 'How—how long is Adam likely to be in hospital?'

Nick glanced at Beth. 'I'd say it could be about ten days—two weeks, maybe. Depending on the test results, of course, and how he responds to treatment.'

'Oh, no. We were due to fly home tomorrow. We're supposed to vacate the hotel room. And what about the expense if we have to stay here? How will we get home afterwards?'

'Look, don't worry about that now,' Beth said evenly. 'I'm sure something can be arranged. You have holiday insurance?'

'Well, yes.'

'Then I'm sure everything will be taken care of.' She smiled reassuringly. 'We'll get someone to contact the company and arrange accommodation for you.'

'I want to be with Adam.'

'Yes, of course you do, and that's fine. But when he's feeling a little better you'll need some space.' Beth smiled at Maggie. 'Staff Nurse here will help you with all the details. You don't need to worry about a thing. And when Adam is feeling better, she'll help you to make arrangements through the insurance company for a flight home.'

'Right now we need to get the tests done so that we can start Thomas on a course of treatment.' Nick smiled. 'Look, why don't you take a break? I'm sure you must be exhausted. Have a cup of coffee while we make Adam comfortable on the ward, then you can come back and sit with him.'

Maggie took her cue and gently led the tearful woman away. Nick moved away from the examination couch and Beth followed, lowering her voice as she said softly, 'He's quite poorly, isn't he?'

Washing his hands he nodded grimly. 'He's young, only five. If it *is* bacterial pneumonia, and I'm pretty sure it is, we need to get him started on antibiotics as soon as possible.'

'I'll see to it now.'

She turned away, pausing fractionally as he said, 'Thanks, Beth.'

'I didn't do anything.'

'You were here. I appreciate it.' He looked away, engrossed in his notes. 'I'll see you later.'

She didn't answer. She didn't even want to think about it. What was it they said? Out of sight out of mind? Except that, in the case of Nick D'Angelo, somehow she had the feeling that it wouldn't work that way. She didn't know anything about him, except that he had walked, uninvited, into her life and that he seemed to provoke a great many conflicting emotions in her, none of which made for an easy working relationship.

CHAPTER FIVE

BETH had drawn the curtains in her apartment, shutting out the light. She was sitting in the chair, her feet tucked under her, when the doorbell rang again, more insistently this time, as if the caller was becoming impatient. Sighing, she finally rose to her feet and went to answer it, guessing that if she didn't Nick was perfectly capable of standing there all night if necessary, ringing the bell.

He looked at her, his dark gaze narrowing as they raked her pale face. 'Why didn't you answer? You must have heard me ringing.'

'Yes, I heard you. It would have been difficult not to,' she said resentfully. 'As a matter of fact, I was hoping that if I kept you waiting long enough you might give up and go away.'

He seemed amused. 'You underrate me. I don't give up that easily.'

She sighed. 'No, somehow I didn't imagine that you would.'

'So, may I come in? Or do you wish me to wait here while you get your jacket?'

She stood back, holding the door open. 'You'd…better come in. The sitting room is through here. It's not very large, I'm afraid.'

He walked past her into the sitting room. He was wearing a lightweight, expensively cut suit, which emphasised the breadth of his shoulders and made the most of his long, lean frame. Beth gazed up at him and wished she hadn't. A six-foot-and-then-some man in a small sitting room could be a problem in more ways than one!

His gaze tracked lazily over her face. 'So, why weren't you going to answer the door? And, more to the point...' he looked at the jeans and T-shirt she was wearing '...why aren't you ready? Or had you forgotten we have a dinner arrangement?'

'No, I hadn't forgotten. I changed my mind.'

'I see. You mean you've chickened out?'

'No!' She moistened her dry lips with her tongue.

A flicker of concern flashed over the handsome features. His glance shifted to take in the drawn curtains and the chair with its crumpled cushions where she had obviously been resting her head.

'Are you ill, Beth?' he rasped anxiously.

'No, I'm fine.'

He frowned. 'Then perhaps you can explain.'

'There's nothing to explain.' She gritted her teeth. 'I thought it was a woman's prerogative to change her mind.'

His gaze narrowed questioningly. 'You are cross.'

She gave a short laugh. 'You could say.'

'Are you going to tell me why?'

'What did you say to James?' She flung the challenge at him.

'I don't know. What *did* I say to James?'

She glared at him. 'This isn't funny.'

'No, I see that it isn't,' he said gravely. 'But if I have offended—'

'You told James that you had spoken to me this morning, *before* you left for the hospital.'

'*Si.*' He frowned. 'But this is true.'

'And James knows that you were at my apartment last night when he phoned.'

'*Si.*' He looked at her, seeing the faint flush suddenly darkening her cheeks. 'And this is also true. But...' He frowned, then his gaze narrowed. 'Ah, I begin to see.'

She glared intently at the attractive planes of his face, looking for some sign of amusement at her expense. His mouth was nerve-shatteringly sensual.

She drew herself up sharply. 'James thought... He got the impression...'

A spasm flickered briefly over his features. 'I am not responsible for your lover's thoughts, *cara.*'

Her gaze flew up to meet his. 'James is *not* my lover.'

'No?' He raised one dark eyebrow and drawled softly. 'Poor James. He is jealous, perhaps?'

Beth choked. 'No, he is not jealous.'

'*I* would be jealous, *cara*, if you were mine and I thought another man had looked at you,' he said softly. She felt an odd fluttering sensation begin in her stomach, as his hands reached out to gently trace the curve of her arms before he drew her slowly towards him. 'I would be very jealous.'

She saw a muscle tighten in his jaw then slowly he released her and looked at his watch. 'It's getting late. You'd better go and get changed.'

She swallowed hard. 'I'm still not at all sure that I want to go out with you.'

'We still have to talk, Beth. Neither of us have eaten. Unless, of course, you would prefer to talk here.'

She knew she was fighting a losing battle. 'I'll go and get changed, but only on condition that you remember this is strictly business.'

'I always keep my word, Beth.' Amusement threaded his voice. 'Besides, I'm sure you'll agree, there is safety in numbers.'

She threw him a scathing look before heading for the bedroom where, sitting in front of the mirror, she brushed her hair until it fell in soft waves against her face. She applied a light covering of make-up, her green eyes, framed by thick, dark lashes, needing little emphasis. Finally, having studied the contents of her wardrobe, she settled for something suitably neutral, not too dressy, not too informal. She chose a sleeveless, knee-length linen dress with a matching jacket. The fact that the dress moulded itself to her body, emphasising her tiny waist and slender hips, was something of which she was completely unaware as she stared at her reflection in the long mirror. She applied a touch of her favourite perfume, slipped her feet into a pair of high-heeled sandals, then took a deep breath, nerving herself to walk into the sitting room.

She hesitated in the open doorway. 'Can I offer you a drink before we go?' she asked Nick. 'I'm afraid I don't keep much alcohol, just a little brandy for visitors...' She broke off, aware of his penetrating gaze raking her slowly from head to toe, lingering with disturbing intensity on the curve of her breasts, the narrowness of her waist and hips.

Panic hit her. He didn't like the dress? She stared down at it. 'Is...is something wrong—with the dress, I mean?' Was it maybe a little too plain—too businesslike? She passed her tongue over her dry lips. 'I could always go and change.'

'You look beautiful, *cara*,' Nick said softly. 'I think we'd better forget the drink.'

She glanced anxiously at her watch. 'I hadn't realised we were late.'

'We're not—*yet*,' he said tautly.

Beth swallowed hard, her breathing uneven as he ushered her outside and to his car, opening the passenger door and helping her in before going round to the driver's side. It wasn't a small car, but he was still too close. She could feel the warmth of his body against hers, smell the distinctive aftershave he was wearing.

'So, what's this place like then where we're going?' she asked as he concentrated on edging out into the traffic.

'Oh, somewhere small, where the food is not just something on a plate but is something prepared with love. The waiters don't hover, and the music is not loud.' He turned his head to look at her. 'It's a family business. Italian, of course. Owned and run by Antonio and his wife Donatella. You do like Italian food?'

'I love it. Most of it anyway, especially when—as you say—it's cooked and prepared by someone who actually cares about what they're doing.'

'Good. In that case, I'm sure you'll enjoy it.'

But it wasn't the food she was worried about!

Beth deliberately turned her head to stare out of the window. Nick seemed far too sure of himself and of what would please her. However, she couldn't resist a tiny gasp of pleasure as the car drew up outside the restaurant.

Inside, it was already busy. An abundance of wonderful smells—garlic and mushrooms and spicy cheeses—assailed Beth's nostrils, and although she had told herself she wasn't hungry she was surprised to feel her stomach rumble.

Their arrival was greeted by the head waiter who, from the way he rushed towards them, hands outstretched, obviously recognised Nick.

'My old friend! Is good to see you again. Where have you been so long? We missed you.'

'You know how it is, Marco. Always busy.'

'Ah!' The young Italian raised his hands. 'Always busy. Still, a man must eat.'

Nick laughed and Beth watched, intrigued, as the two men continued to exchange greetings before they were led to a secluded table. A candle flickered and there were fresh flowers on the table. It all spoke of an intimacy that brought a sudden and unexpected tightness to her throat, so that she hesitated momentarily.

'Is something wrong?' The faint note of concern in Nick's voice drew her up with a start.

'What? Oh, no.' She sat quickly in the chair Marco was holding out for her. 'This is lovely. It's not quite what I'd expected for a business meeting, that's all.'

His mouth quirked. 'There's no rule which says business must be formal and unenjoyable. Neither of us have eaten and I enjoy the food here.' He looked at her. 'We could easily have gone somewhere more private. Would you have preferred that?'

'No.' Beth almost choked on the word. She was

conscious of the hint of laughter in his voice. 'This is fine.'

She smiled at Marco who had returned with the menus, and focused her attention deliberately on the pages. After a few moments, to Nick's obvious amusement, she had to admit defeat. 'I'm sorry, there's so much to choose from and it all sounds wonderful.'

'In that case, will you trust me to choose something for you? Or is that asking too much?'

She gave a wry smile. 'Since we're only talking about food, I'm more than happy to accept your judgement. I'm not difficult to please.'

His eyes darkened to fathomless brown pools. 'Oh, but I'd say you were very discerning, Beth. A little cautious—afraid—maybe. But when you find the courage to spread your wings, I'm sure the results will be far more rewarding than you could ever have imagined.'

She blushed furiously as she realised he had deliberately given a double meaning to the words. 'I was talking about the food.'

'I didn't imagine otherwise.'

She watched as he gave their order to Marco then listened, fascinated, as the two men lapsed into Italian. For the first time, as she watched them laughing together, she saw Nick completely at ease. It was only as both men turned to look at her that she guessed she had become the subject of their conversation, and she smiled nervously, waiting until Marco had taken their order and left before saying defensively, 'What did he say? I heard my name mentioned but I couldn't understand all of the conversation.'

'You don't speak Italian?'

'Yes, of course. Or, at least, I get by. The majority of our patients are British or French, so unfortunately I don't get as much chance to practise my language skills as you might think.'

He grinned. 'It was friendly chit-chat, that's all. I asked about his family. Marco has a great many brothers, sisters, cousins, aunts... He was telling me he plans to marry next year. In return I felt it would have been churlish not to satisfy his curiosity about us.'

'He must have been disappointed. After all, there's nothing to tell him, is there?'

'Please, don't be offended,' he said quickly. 'We Italians love our families. Our lives are intertwined. We enjoy being together. I suppose it makes us naturally curious about other people's lives.' He smiled. 'We like to ask questions, and when we know all about you, you become a friend for life.'

Beth toyed with her empty glass. 'So, what did you tell him?'

'It scarcely matters what I told him. Like most Italians, Marco is a romantic. He sees a beautiful girl in terms of a wife and mother to children. I explained that the British are more reserved.'

'And what about you?' She put the question and realised she felt suddenly shy as he looked at her through the halo of light from the candle. 'I mean...I'm just curious to know how you came to be working at the hospital? Why medicine?'

He shrugged. 'Let's just say there is a family connection. My maternal grandmother was British. She came to Italy to stay with friends in order to convalesce after an illness, and during her stay she was introduced to my grandfather. They fell in love, and the rest, as they say, is history.'

She smiled. 'Do you see much of your parents?'

It was as if a shutter came down over the dark eyes, and she was shocked by the sudden tensing of his hands. 'No. My mother was killed in a car accident when I was eight years old.'

Beth felt her heart give a painful jolt. 'So you were raised by your father.'

'No. He had a heart attack four years after my mother died. It was a shock to everyone. He was young and had always seemed so fit. He liked sport, played tennis, swam. One day he was fine and the next…he was gone.' The hand Beth reached out to him was held for a few brief seconds then released. 'I remember feeling stunned, dazed, asking why. How could it happen? I'm sure the family tried to explain, but I was a child. How could I understand?'

Unthinkingly, she reached out again and his fingers closed over hers once more. 'I'm so sorry. It must have been awful for you.'

He gave a slight smile. 'It was a long time ago, and the memories I have of them both are all good. I was taken into the family, raised by a grandfather I idolise. He is a doctor, too. I think that's why I made the decision to follow in his footsteps. There were dozens of uncles and aunts and cousins to see to it that I didn't suffer for the loss. So one thing I don't need is pity.'

'I wasn't aware that I had offered any.'

He leaned forward, frowning. 'Then what is it, Beth?'

She flicked him a quick, nervous glance, and was saved the necessity of a reply by the arrival of their food. It served as an excuse to relieve the tension which had suddenly sparked between them.

'Mmm, this looks good. What is it?'

'This is just the starter—antipasto. Rounds of bread with various toppings—spicy cheese, chopped chicken livers, porcini mushrooms.' He studied the wine list. 'Do you have any particular preference for red or white wine?'

She fumbled with her knife. 'I don't drink.'

'Everyone drinks, Beth.'

'I mean, I don't drink alcohol.'

'Is that for a particular reason?' He ordered Chianti and a glass of fruit juice before lifting his gaze to study her troubled face.

'I simply happen to prefer non-alcoholic drinks, that's all,' she said firmly.

'Well, I hope you approve of the food. I've ordered chicken to follow, stewed in red wine, onions, tomatoes and garlic.'

Beth was surprised to find that she had suddenly developed an appetite. 'You were right,' she conceded a little later. 'That was lovely.'

Nick sat back, waiting for the second course to be served. 'Perhaps you should have more spirit of adventure. It suits you.'

Two small spots of colour swam into her cheeks. 'I prefer to be cautious about most new things. I find it far safer.'

'Nothing is safe for ever, Beth. Sooner or later you'll have to come out from behind those barriers you've built around yourself and face the world. The alternative is to spend your life alone. But perhaps if you're scared enough you'll end up doing just that.'

Her eyes were stormy as she looked at him across the table. 'Why should you care what I do with my life?'

'Because I hate waste, and I do have an interest.'

She stared down at her plate and picked up her fork to toy with her food. 'Let's just get one thing clear, shall we? As far as I'm concerned, the only interest we can ever possibly have in common is work, and I prefer to keep it that way. That *is* why you brought me here? To discuss business? If not, I can easily leave.' She had already half risen from her chair when his hand closed over her wrist.

'Damn it, sit down and eat your food.' Anger blazed from Nick's dark eyes. 'Antonio and Donatella are my friends. I won't have them thinking their hospitality isn't to your liking simply because you have some imagined grievance against me.'

Beth pulled away from his restraining hand on her arm, breathing hard. 'You said it was business. You gave your word.'

'And I intend to keep it.' He drew a harsh breath.

She swallowed convulsively, tautly aware of the sheer physical magnetism of this man, the cool, almost frightening determination.

'Please.'

She sank down shakily.

Marco hovered, his expression troubled. 'Is everything all right? The food...?'

'Is wonderful, thank you, Marco. Please, tell your mother her cooking is superb.'

Beth couldn't bring herself to look at Nick. 'I

thought I'd lost my bag and panicked, but it's here.' She showed him the slim bag and Marco smiled.

'Ah, good. But, still, be on your guard against pickpockets.' He went away happy.

'Thank you,' Nick said. 'Marco and I have been friends for a long time. I wouldn't wish to see him upset.'

Beth made yet another attempt to eat, pushing the food round her plate. 'I'm sorry, it looks delicious but—'

'No.' His mouth tightened. '*I* am sorry. Where you are concerned, it seems I still have a lot to learn about self-control, and I'm not finding it easy.' He seemed to share her own lack of appetite, and reached for his wine instead. 'So...let's talk business,' he rasped.

Beth looked across the table, confused by his sudden withdrawal. 'Nick...'

'You did say you'd read the report I left with you, outlining some of the thoughts I have about future developments?'

'I said I'd skimmed through it. It was fairly lengthy.'

'In spite of not being interested?' His smile was deliberately provocative again, yet somehow she felt more at ease with that than his anger.

'I haven't said I'm not interested in your ideas.'

'Just that you would prefer not to work for me.' He picked up his fork again. 'Which is good, because I had in mind that you would work *with* me. So, give me your thoughts on the report.'

She frowned. 'You seem to have a lot of ideas— very ambitious ideas.'

'And you disapprove of ambition?'

'I didn't say that.'

'But you think that because The Hermitage is a relatively small hospital we should not be ambitious?' He shook his head. 'The hospital may be state-owned, but it is privately funded, Beth. It must pay its way, and it will do that better if we offer better, more modern services.'

'Yes, I accept that...'

'Cardiac care, to give just one example, has moved on. The equipment we have is old and outdated. It needs to be replaced and the department expanded. The need is there. Many of our patients are elderly. We could do more in the way of preventive medicine—well women's clinics. Clinics for men, screening against testicular cancer. And I believe we should expand the rheumatology clinic.' He looked at her. 'I can see there is a need. I would also like to open the hospital up to non-fee-paying patients, though I know it may be controversial.'

'It all sounds very well...'

'We can't go on simply treating very rich patients or dealing with insurance cases, Beth. There's more to medicine than that. We owe something to the local community.'

'Yes, I agree. But how do you know the sponsors will back you? What you're suggesting will cost money—a lot of money.'

'I think I can persuade them.'

She didn't doubt it for a moment. 'I have to ask—' she looked at him steadily '—why are you telling *me* this? There must be other people far better qualified.' She frowned. 'Surely you should be discussing this with James. He has seniority. You must know that he always expected—hoped—to take over from Max.'

Nick sat back in his chair and looked at her. 'James has a grand vision for the future.'

'He's a very good doctor.'

'I agree. I know this, having spoken to James, briefly, and to members of the staff. James has a vision for *his* future. But what I'm looking for is someone with a vision for this hospital, someone uninhibited by years of tradition who won't dismiss a new idea on the grounds that it was always done a different way, so why change the system? I've seen the way you work. You're a good doctor, caring and perceptive. I haven't just seen that for myself, I've heard others say it. I know where you did your medical training. I also know that you were considered to be the best medical student in your group, and that you passed your finals with honours.'

Beth gasped. 'You've been checking up on me.'

'But of course.' He laughed. 'I do have the safety of our patients to consider.'

'But why me? I mean, where exactly is all this leading?'

'I had hoped it might be obvious. I am offering you a job, Beth. What I am looking for is someone with a feel for the way we live here, not simply for the medicine but for the job. Someone who understands the Italian temperament.'

She gave a slight laugh. 'I'm not sure that I do.'

'Oh, I think so, Beth. Which is why I am asking you to be my deputy.'

She felt her heartbeat quicken as their eyes met across the table. She tried to look away but couldn't.

His eyes held hers and refused to let go, making her, for the first time, aware of that side of him which was timeless, inherited from his ancestors.

'But I already have a job, and I really don't know Italy all that well. I work here and I love it, but I still don't think that makes me ideal for the job you have in mind.'

'The idea scares you?' asked Nick quietly.

'No.' Her head went up. 'I'm not afraid of responsibility.'

'Then what is it, Beth? Or need I ask?'

'Probably not.' Her tone was sharp as she looked at him. 'But if you want me to be honest…'

'But of course.'

'Then I don't think I want to work with you.'

He gave an exasperated sigh. 'You realise what you would be turning down?'

'Yes.' She bit at her lip. 'I think so.'

'And you can dismiss it so easily?'

She stared into the depths of her glass. 'Not easily, no. I'm flattered, of course, but—'

'I wasn't looking to flatter you. I see you as someone with dedication and vision. Perhaps I was wrong, if you think of refusing for reasons which are strictly personal.' He looked at her over the rim of his glass and said huskily, 'Because you know that I find you beautiful. Does it trouble you, Beth? To know that I want you?'

She moistened her dry lips with her tongue. 'That isn't possible. You don't even know me.'

A muscle pulsed in his jaw. 'I know that you've been hurt. But you have to learn to let go, Beth,' he urged softly. 'I would never hurt you.'

Not intentionally maybe, she thought. She felt the breath catch in her throat as he leaned forward, cupping her face, bringing her so close that her nostrils were invaded by the familiar smell of him.

Shock briefly widened her eyes at the realisation that he was going to kiss her—and it hazily registered on her shell-shocked mind that she wanted him to. The sensual mouth was just a breath away.

Moaning softly, she swayed towards him. For an instant she closed her eyes, telling herself this shouldn't be happening. For an instant she felt him tense, then he set her free, his breathing harsh as he drew away, leaving her senses reeling in confusion. She started to speak then became dizzyingly aware of Marco standing beside the table, anxiously surveying the barely touched plates of food.

'Is everything all right? You don't like the food? I take away and bring you something else?' He was already looking for a menu.

'No. No, thank you, Marco.' Nick smiled. 'The food is fine. We were simply...having a breather. Isn't that right, Beth?'

She felt the brilliant colour flame into her cheeks. 'Oh, yes. The food is fine, Marco.'

'*Bene.* Ah, but your glasses are nearly empty.' Before she could prevent it, he had refilled Nick's glass with wine and her own with fruit juice, smiling as he replaced the bottle and hurried away to attend to new customers.

Nick gave a wry smile. 'I am sorry.'

'Don't be.' She cleared her throat, 'After all, we are here to talk business.'

'Ah, yes. Business. It is far safer, no?'

Far safer, yes. She batted the thought away. 'So, where were we, before…'

'I was asking you to become my deputy, and you were considering it. Obviously we'll need to discuss and exchange ideas. What I have in mind will mean some fairly big changes. I imagine you'll want to put forward your own views. Is that so difficult?'

She eyed him warily, relieved that the tension which had sparked between them had been broken. 'I don't know. I hadn't even considered anything like this.'

Nick frowned. 'The simple truth is, Beth, that either we move with the times or we close. It really is as simple as that.'

'You're not serious?'

'I don't joke about such things. The sponsors won't support a lost cause. You can hardly blame them. So it's up to us to make it happen.'

'And that's all you want? My signature on a contract?'

'I'll settle for that—for now. In the meantime, I'd like you to draft a comprehensive report of areas where you think changes and improvements might be made. Budgets we can go into later. Obviously I shall need to put the whole thing before the board of sponsors.'

She eyed him directly. 'Does this mean there's a chance I might get a new hydrotherapy pool for my rheumatology patients? Some of them have such limited mobility because of their swollen, painful joints, yet the minute they get into the warm water they can move freely.'

'You don't have to sell the idea to me, Beth. Do your homework. Put your case to the sponsors.'

'It all *sounds* reasonable.'

'There aren't any catches, if that's what you mean. We both have the best interests of the hospital and its patients at heart. Shall we shake hands on a deal, or perhaps you'd prefer to seal it with a kiss?'

She bit back a response as Marco came to remove their plates before returning to flourish the menus yet again.

'I really don't think I can manage a dessert.' She smiled at him.

'Oh, but you must try something—just a little. Mamma makes the very good dessert.'

She could see it was an argument she wasn't going to win. 'Well, in that case... Now, this sounds very nice.'

Marco followed her pointing finger, nodding his approval. 'Ah, yes. Tiramisu. Is the delicate sponge, the coffee, a little liqueur.' He kissed his fingertips. 'Is wonderful, especially the way Mamma makes.' He made a little moue of doubt. 'Is *very* sweet.'

Beth snapped the menu to a close. 'In that case, it will do very nicely for Dr D'Angelo. His temper needs all the sweetening it can get. I'll just have the coffee—without sugar. Thank you, Marco.'

She heard Nick make a soft choking sound in his throat as Marco ambled away, laughing softly to himself.

'Happy now?' Nick growled.

'Not yet, but I'm getting there,' she glared at him. Behind the candle glow she sensed that he smiled.

'Can I take this to mean we have a truce, and that you'll sign the contract?'

'Have you even considered the possibility that I might let you down? You're taking a risk.'

'I don't think so. As I said, you're a good doctor. You have the vision to see what needs to be done, and I don't think you'll be afraid to make decisions, even if they might be unpopular.'

'You make me sound ruthless—like you.'

'Sometimes it is necessary to be a little ruthless in order to achieve what must be done.' His eyes darkened. 'I have faith in you, Beth. I know that you will give me what I want, sooner or later. I am a patient man. I am prepared to wait until you can learn to trust me.'

She looked at him and felt a sensation of pure excitement run through her. She could deny it as much as she liked, but the sheer sensuality, the animal magnetism of him sent a wave of desire running through her body.

'Nick, I...'

He frowned then, very slowly, his expression changed to one of wonderment. 'Beth?'

'No, please, don't.' She tried to evade the hand that imprisoned her own. 'I don't understand what's happening. I'm confused.'

'I'd never hurt you, you must know that,' he rasped. 'Trust me. Is that so difficult?'

She shook her head. 'I do trust you.' The trouble was, it was already too late. She was already hurting in a way she had promised herself she would never hurt again.

She barely tasted the strong black coffee Marco

placed before her. Nick left untouched the dessert she had ordered. He said something in Italian to Marco as he paid the bill, then his hand was under her arm as he escorted her out to the car.

The air was still warm, but a refreshing breeze brought welcome relief from the day's earlier heat.

'It was a lovely meal,' she said after he had closed the door behind her and gone round to the driver's seat. 'Thank you. I enjoyed the evening.'

'You didn't expect to?' He eased the car deftly into the traffic. 'You didn't eat much.'

'I wasn't very hungry.' Beth opened the window to let the breeze cool her cheeks, but it did nothing to lessen the tension which seemed to crackle between them like electricity.

Ten minutes later they drew to a halt outside Beth's apartment. Nick switched off the engine and cut the lights. The air outside was still warm and it needed a real effort to climb out. One way or another it had been quite a day, and suddenly Beth felt reluctant to enter the silence of the apartment. The last thing she needed right now was to be alone with her thoughts.

'Well, I suppose...' She sighed involuntarily.

Instantly, Nick's gaze narrowed. 'Beth, don't go.'

'It's getting late.'

She heard his soft intake of breath as his hands came down on her shoulders, drawing her gently towards him, and she was shaken by the riot of emotions that coursed through her as, with slow deliberation, he took her in his arms.

'Don't be afraid, Beth.'

Easily said, but he didn't know the dangers. She closed her eyes as his finger gently traced the curve of her cheek, and she felt her breath falter as his mouth came ever closer, tantalising her with its warm desirability so that her own lips parted on a groan of frustration.

She must have been crazy to think she could remain indifferent. The kiss seemed to plunder her senses, stripping away the frail barriers of resistance she had built around her. Desire coursed through her. She was appalled by her own weakness where he was concerned. What about her loyalty to Paul? Didn't it count for anything? the voice of her conscience jibed. But she had never felt this way about Paul.

She said hoarsely, 'No, Nick, I... Please, don't.'

He moaned softly against her hair, releasing her mouth for an instant only to reclaim it again, more brutally this time, as if sensing her reluctance ebbing away.

Don't let it stop, some inner voice pleaded. Don't ever let it stop. Her hands reached up, her fingers twining hungrily in the silky softness of his hair.

'I want you, *amore mio*.' His voice was hoarse. 'You must know that.'

She didn't want to fight the sense of urgency which was threatening to engulf her. It had been so long since her body had felt this kind of need, this kind of hunger. It would be so easy to let go.

'I need you, Beth,' he said thickly. His hands ran gently through her hair, moved to her shoulders, followed the curve of her breasts, sending tremors of excitement down her spine. 'You want me as much as I want you. You're only kidding yourself if you think otherwise.'

It wasn't true, she told herself. She wouldn't let it

be true. She shook her head, pushing weakly against him.

'You can lie to yourself if you want to,' he said huskily, 'but not to me, *cara*. No one could respond as you do in my arms and not feel something. I can feel the way you tremble.'

'That's...that's because I don't want you to touch me.'

'You can't run away for ever, Beth,' he muttered harshly. 'Sooner or later you're going to have to let go—let the past go. There's a whole new future out there. All you have to do is reach out. It's yours for the taking.'

'No.' Beth's fingers dug into the fine fabric of his shirt, feeling the powerful muscle beneath. Yes, she wanted him, but she had been down this road before, and it only led to pain. She was afraid...afraid to let go...to love again.

Love. The realisation shocked her. Was this really love? If so, it seemed to bear no comparison to what she had felt for Paul.

She shook her head as a feeling of panic rose, threatening to engulf her. She had thought herself in love once before, and it had brought nothing but grief. She had vowed she would never go through that again.

What she was feeling now couldn't be love, she tried to tell herself. Nick had come into her life when she was still vulnerable, that was all. He had made her aware of emotions and sensations which she had never experienced before, not even with Paul. He hadn't even said he loved her. Needed, yes. Wanted.

But love? Was it any wonder she felt confused—way out of her depth?

'What are you so afraid of, Beth?' Nick's breath fanned gently against her cheek.

'Nothing. I don't know what you mean. I must go. It's late.'

'You must know I'd never do anything to hurt you. I want you, Beth. I need you in my life.'

A sob caught in her throat and she stiffened in his arms. She tried to drag herself away and felt his arms tighten, saw the look of confusion in his eyes.

'Beth, what is it?'

'No, please, don't.' She closed her eyes, aware of the turmoil in Nick's eyes as she broke free, panicking as she realised how little it would take to make her surrender. If he kissed her again…

'I can't. I won't be hurt again. I've been through it and I don't intend to let it happen again, not a second time.'

Nick released her abruptly, his face taut as he looked at her. 'Some day it may happen, and you won't be able to fight it. You have to start trusting someone some time.'

She pressed a shaking hand to her mouth. 'I won't let it.' The words were whispered as he drew away, but she thought in sudden terror that it was already too late. She was already in love with Nick.

'I don't give up so easily, Beth.'

'You have no choice,' she said dully. She pushed open the car door and climbed out. 'Goodnight.'

'I'll be in touch.'

It sounded almost like a warning but she chose to ignore it. She let herself into the apartment and shut the door behind her, leaning her head back against the solid wood. She felt incredibly tired, more tired than she had for a very long time, and somehow she didn't think her state of mind had anything to do with memories of Paul.

CHAPTER SIX

IF ANYTHING, the temperature outside was even hotter during the following week. Tempers frayed, tourists sunbathed and suffered the consequences. In a way, Beth thought, it was almost a relief to be kept busy.

Where Nick was concerned, caution had become the watchword of Beth's day, and it seemed she had succeeded, until she walked into her apartment one night and flicked the button on the answering-machine. Suddenly his voice seemed to follow her, stopping her in her tracks as she headed for the kitchen.

'Beth, I need that report you were going to let me have. I'm seeing the sponsors fairly soon and I shall need to put figures in front of them. I shall be at Medics International headquarters tomorrow at one. Meet me there, will you?'

She stood for several seconds battling against a feeling panic. She had known she couldn't avoid him for ever, but she wasn't ready—not yet—not when she only had to hear his voice for her heart to start leaping crazily. How could she possibly face him tomorrow?

Beth walked through to the small kitchen, flipped the switch on the electric kettle to make herself a cup of coffee and reached for her diary. She was shocked to discover that her hands were shaking as she turned the pages, and then almost laughed with relief as she realised that she already had an appointment for the following day. A legitimate excuse—a breathing space. Nick had said he didn't give up easily. She had hoped he would and then had prayed that he wouldn't! Either way, she wasn't ready to deal with this, not yet.

She carried her diary into the sitting room and reached for the phone. Dialling his number, she waited, moistening her dry lips with her tongue as she rehearsed what she would say. She could hear the tone ringing. Illogically she could imagine him sitting by the phone, refusing to pick it up.

'Come on!' she muttered.

Frustrated, she replaced the receiver, made herself a strong black cup of coffee, then dialled the number again, with the same result. With a sigh of impatience she was just about to replace the receiver again, then jumped as the answering-machine clicked on.

'I'm sorry,' an anonymous voice explained. 'Dr D'Angelo is unavailable right now. If you would care to leave a message...'

Beth swallowed hard. 'Nick, this is Beth. I got your message. I'm sorry, I can't make the meeting tomorrow. Can we reschedule? Get back to me, will you?'

If nothing else, it meant she had avoided seeing Nick, although she was well aware that she was merely postponing the inevitable. But at least this way, when it happened, she would be more composed, better prepared.

She walked into the office the following morning, dropping a bundle of files on to the desk before sinking with a sigh of relief into a chair. Several restless nights' sleep hadn't done much for her peace of mind.

She glanced at her list of messages and frowned. 'Jill, I'm still expecting a call from Dr D'Angelo. Is there a problem? Only I'm due in the rheumatology clinic in about half an hour and I'd hoped to hear from him before then.'

'Sorry, Beth. I'm still trying to contact him for you, but his secretary insists he is unavailable.' Tall, dark-haired and attractive, Jill Duncan had joined the hospital as a medical secretary at about the same time as Beth, and the two had become firm friends over the past few years.

'I see.' Beth frowned. 'OK, thanks, Jill. I appreciate it.'

There was a slight pause as Jill reached for the phone and looked at Beth. 'Do you want me to keep trying?'

Beth smiled. 'No, that's all right. It's a bit late now anyway. It's just that he left a message yesterday, scheduling a meeting for later this morning. He wants to discuss this draft report, but I can't make it. I've another appointment. I returned his message, saying as much and asking if we can postpone.' She glanced at her watch. 'Look, why don't you go for your coffee-break?'

'I really don't mind giving it a miss and trying his number again.'

Beth thought about it and shook her head. 'No, don't worry. I'll sort something out. I just wish he'd given me more notice, that's all.'

'He's probably busy.'

'He's practically uncontactable.'

'Well, I don't know about that. Mind you, I haven't seen him around the hospital for a while, have you?'

'I can't say I've noticed.' Beth deliberately concentrated her gaze on the bundle of case notes she had gathered up from the desk.

'So, what are you going to do?'

'I don't see what I can do.' Beth glanced at the report she had been working on. 'I'll just carry on as usual and assume, since I haven't heard from him, that the meeting has been cancelled. Which is just as well. I'm meeting Grace and I don't want to let her down. I think she needs to talk.'

Jill pulled a wry face. 'What if he didn't get your message for some reason? Isn't he going to be a bit cross if he turns up for the meeting and you're not there? You did say the report was pretty important.'

'I *thought* it was. I've spent the past few days working on it, coming up with figures, until my head's reeling.' She rose to her feet and gathered up the folder. 'I really don't see how I can be held responsible when I wasn't consulted about the arrangement in the first place.' She raked a hand forcibly through her hair. 'Most things I could rearrange, but I really don't want to break this lunch date with Grace. We made the arrangement a week ago, and she leaves the hospital tomorrow for good.'

'Have you tried leaving a message with his secretary, explaining?'

'Yes, of course. I've even tried calling from home, but all I get is the same response. "I'm very sorry," Beth mimicked. "Dr D'Angelo is still unavailable, but the moment he returns to the office…"'

'Mmm. Not much help, is it?' Jill shook her head.

'No, not really.'

Jill gave her a sideways glance. 'Look, would it

help if you left the report with me and I were to deliver it? Just in case…'

Beth looked at her and felt her heart give a momentary leap. 'Would you be able to do that?'

The other woman shrugged. 'I don't see why not. At least, that way, if he does turn up, he can get to read it, and presumably he'll get in touch with you if there are any problems.'

'It would be great if you could.'

'I can't think of another answer, can you? The priority seems to be that he gets the report. Obviously I can't discuss it in detail since I only went through some of the figures with you and typed it up. But at least it will have been delivered.'

Beth hesitated. 'I don't think he's going to be wildly happy with some of the suggestions I've made. Expanding the rheumatology department alone is going to be expensive, especially if we get the hydrotherapy pool I've been asking for, but we do need it. He's bound to come up with questions.'

'In which case, I'll answer them to the best of my ability whilst pointing out that you had an urgent prior engagement. Is that the report?'

'Yes, but… Why couldn't he just have answered my call?' Beth bit at her lower lip. 'Look, I'm still not sure…'

'Oh, come on. He can't be such an ogre.'

'I wouldn't count on it.'

In spite of the seriousness of the situation, Beth gave a short laugh. 'I suppose I could always send it by special courier, but I doubt if he'd be impressed.'

'I'll deal with it.' Jill smiled as Beth handed it over.

'And what do you want me to say if he suggests setting up another meeting?'

'Tell him a little notice would be nice.'

Jill chuckled. 'I think I'd better go before I change my mind. Give my regards to Grace, by the way, and tell her I hope the new job works out.'

'I'll do that.'

'See you later.'

Beth waved, and five minutes later, shrugging herself into a short-sleeved white coat, she headed along the corridor.

'Hi.' Smiling, Maggie fell into step beside Beth. She looked cool and attractive in her pale blue, short-sleeved uniform. 'I haven't seen you around for a couple of days. I was beginning to think you'd left us.'

'Hah! Fat chance. I've been busy. I don't like writing reports at the best of times, especially when I'm pressured. I have enough paperwork to deal with as it is.'

Maggie laughed. 'I know the feeling.' Then, more seriously, she said, 'Is there any news on young Adam Bates? He was quite poorly.'

'Yes, he was. I'm just on my way over there now. It must be a worrying time for his parents.'

'Weren't they supposed to be flying home a few days ago?'

'Yes, I gather so. I'm afraid they've had to do quite a lot of rearranging of their plans. Let's hope I can give them some more positive news today.'

'I'll cross my fingers for you. Oh, by the way, have you looked in on Alice Craig recently?'

'Yes, last night, as a matter of fact. She seems to be making good progress.'

'I know. Her husband was certainly looking happier first thing this morning.' She grinned. 'Right, then. I'm off to Casualty. See you later.'

Beth waved before turning and heading for the small private room where Adam lay in bed. He was asleep, and Beth was pleased to see that the flush had gone from his cheeks and he was breathing more easily.

Sue Bates was sitting in a chair, watching her small son. A discarded English newspaper lay on the bedside cabinet, along with a half-empty paper cup of coffee. She glanced up as Beth walked into the room.

'Oh, hello, Doctor. I didn't realise you'd be seeing Adam this morning. He's just fallen asleep.'

'That's all right.' Beth smiled reassuringly as she reached for the clipboard at the end of the bed, already making a quick professional assessment of the child. 'He's certainly starting to look a lot more comfortable.'

'Oh, he is. The nurse said his temperature is down and he isn't as restless.'

'Well, that's a good sign. Let's see what else has been happening.' Beth scanned the notes and flipped the page. 'Is he still complaining of pain under his ribs?'

'No. I mean, he's not exactly happy...'

'No, I'm sure he isn't.' Beth grinned. 'I can't say I blame him, poor little chap. He was quite poorly when you brought him in.'

'But he *is* getting better, isn't he?'

'Yes, he is. There was a large amount of fluid on

his lungs, which is why he was so poorly and uncomfortable.'

'It is pneumonia, isn't it?'

'Yes, that's right.' Beth read the notes. 'But the intravenous antibiotics have certainly helped to make him feel better.'

Sue gently brushed a hand against her son's forehead. 'I was worried to death,' she said shakily. 'I really thought...I thought I was going to lose him.'

Beth smiled sympathetically. 'Yes, I can imagine. These past few days must have been an awful time for you, but happily he's definitely on the mend now.'

The woman glanced up at Beth. 'Does that mean I'll be able to take him home soon?'

'Well, not quite yet. He's still going to need antibiotics for a while, and we'd like to see his temperature fully back to normal. I'll just have a listen to his chest while I'm here.' Beth applied her stethoscope gently to the sleeping child's chest before nodding and straightening up. 'Yes, that definitely sounds much better. Has he eaten anything yet?'

'Not much.'

'No, but I don't suppose I'd feel like eating either if I were Adam. As long as he drinks plenty of fluids I'm not too worried.'

'When do you think I'll be able to take him home, then?'

'Oh, I'd say in about another week.'

'A week!'

'I know. It can't be easy for you, spending most of your time at the hospital in this small room. But I promise you, you'll see him improve a little more every day, and you really should try to go out and get a little fresh air for a while. Just a stroll, maybe. Adam will be fine, you know, and the nurses will make sure he's looked after.'

'Oh, yes, I know…'

'You need to look after yourself as well,' Beth said gently. 'Go and get a proper meal. Take some time off to relax, even if it's only an hour.'

'Well…' Sue smiled wryly. 'I must admit, I am beginning to find this room a bit claustrophobic.'

'I'll have a word with the nurse.' Beth smiled and replaced the clipboard at the end of the bed. 'Go out for a couple of hours now, while he's sleeping.'

'I think I might just do that.'

Minutes later, Beth was heading down the corridor. Luckily the rheumatology clinic was fairly quiet for once. Probably, she guessed, because a number of her regular patients were away on holiday with their families now that the local schools were closed for the summer.

Smiling, she greeted her first patient. 'Hello, Barry. How are you feeling today?'

'Much better, thanks, Doctor.'

'The tablets seem to have done the trick, then?'

Twenty-year-old Barry Frazer looked at Beth, then glanced away again. 'Yeah. I reckon.'

'That's good. I'll just take a look at your knees. It was the left knee that was giving you so much pain, wasn't it?'

'That's right.' He was wearing shorts, and he raised one tanned leg.

'Oh, yes. I can see the swelling has gone down.' She made a gentle but thorough examination. 'What about the other knee?'

'It's fine.'

'Good.' Beth also checked his ankles and feet before getting up to glance at her notes on the computer. Barry had developed arthritis at the age of thirteen. It had started in his feet and had gradually begun to affect his knees and ankles. She could well understand the frustration the condition must have caused, the restrictions it must have placed on a youngster at school, surrounded by his healthier, more mobile classmates.

Barry and his family had moved to Italy six years ago, and he had been referred to her clinic about eighteen months ago after a particularly nasty flare-up of his arthritis.

She smiled. 'You still see the physiotherapist regularly, don't you?'

He nodded but didn't look too happy. 'I don't like it. It's painful when she starts moving my leg.'

'Yes.' She looked sympathetic. 'But it does help. You really do need to keep your joints moving.' She glanced at the computer screen again. 'You've been taking methotrexate for the past seven years?'

'Yeah.' He stared sulkily at his hands.

'Barry, is there a problem? I mean, you *are* taking the medication?'

'Course I am. I don't like it but I take it because I have do, don't I? I don't have any choice.'

Beth was shocked at the sudden note of anger in his voice. She turned to face him. 'Do you want to tell me what the problem is?' she asked gently. 'Perhaps I can help.'

'Hah! I shouldn't think so.'

'You never know. Why don't you give it a try?'

He looked at her, then down at his hands again. 'I just feel so—so frustrated. All I want is to be like the rest of my mates. I want to go out and have a good time—have a few drinks, a few beers or a glass of wine. That's not so much to ask, is it?' His mouth twisted and Beth sensed that he was close to tears. 'I just want to be like everyone else, but because I have to take these damn tablets I can't drink alcohol. How do you think that makes me feel? I'm sick of being different.'

Beth frowned. 'I can understand why you'd feel frustrated about not being able to have a drink with your friends.'

He gave a short laugh. 'Yeah, well—it didn't matter when I was at school, did it? I mean, taking the tablets was something I got used to. It meant the pain wasn't so bad, and I didn't go to the pub then, did I? So being told I mustn't drink alcohol or I couldn't take the tablets didn't matter.'

'And now it does.'

His gaze flicked up to meet hers. 'I've got a girlfriend. We enjoy going to bars.'

'Yes, of course you do.'

'But I'm the only one who can't have an alcoholic drink. I feel like…like a kid.'

Beth drew a deep breath. 'Barry, there's no reason why you can't have a small amount of alcohol.'

He stared at her. 'You're serious? You mean, I can actually have a beer and it won't mean I have to stop taking the tablets?'

'I'm talking about a *small* amount of beer. Would that make a difference?'

'You bet! How much is a small amount?'

She laughed. 'Ah, well, that's what we need to find out. Look, I'll fix up for you to have a chat with our nurse, but I think you'll find that five units of alcohol a week is OK. I do have other patients taking methotrexate, and most of them at one point or another have felt exactly the way you feel. They all ask the same questions. So you aren't alone, if that's any consolation.'

'Oh, yeah!' He grinned. 'You'd be surprised how long I've craved a pint of beer.'

'Well, I'm glad I've managed to cheer you up.'

'You've made my day. OK, so I still have the arthritis. I know it's not going to go away, but at least I feel I can get on with something pretty close to a normal life.'

On which happy note Beth saw him out, wishing her own problems were so easily solved.

Half an hour later, shrugging herself into a blue linen jacket, she drove into town, doing her best to dispel a feeling that she had merely postponed a confrontation with Nick. For the moment, however, with memories of their last meeting still all too fresh in her mind, even this brief respite was something she felt grateful for.

She gave herself a mental shake as she carefully parked her car beneath the shade of a tree, and was actually smiling as she walked into the café where she was to meet Grace.

Beth sat back a few minutes later, having given her order to the waitress.

'I have to say, you look remarkably happy for someone who's supposed to be drowning her sorrows.'

Grace laughed softly. 'Yes, I'm sorry. I suppose I was a bit touchy last time we spoke. How about you, though?' Her gaze was shrewdly appraising. 'Things can't have been too easy for you, what with Max leaving so suddenly. It was a shock for all of us, but especially for you, I suppose. I mean, you have to work so closely with the new man, which can't be easy. I've heard he likes to do things his own way.'

Beth reached for her glass and sipped at the fresh orange juice, resisting the temptation to look at her watch. For some reason, she half expected to see Nick striding across the café towards her, and the thought sent an illogical spasm of panic running through her.

'Oh, things don't seem to be working out too badly, as a matter of fact. He certainly seems to have some new ideas.'

'In that case, perhaps we should be having a double celebration.'

'Double?'

Grace smiled. 'Your promotion and my new job.'

'You sound pleased.'

'I am.'

'But I thought you weren't happy at the possibility of having to leave the hospital.'

'No, I wasn't. But that was before I knew what was on offer.'

Beth smiled. 'And what *is* on offer?'

'I'm being transferred.'

'Transferred?'

'That's right. It seems the sponsors are opening a new clinic about thirty kilometres from here, and they've asked me to take over as Director of Nursing there.'

Beth's eyes widened. 'Grace, that's marvellous!'

'Yes, I know.' The other woman's laugh held a note of embarrassment. 'I reacted pretty badly, didn't I, when the idea of a move was first suggested? But you know what it's like. All sorts of rumours were flying around. I think a lot of us were afraid there wouldn't be a place for us in the new scheme of things.'

'Obviously you're feeling more reassured.'

Grace twirled her glass. 'Well, it helped that our worries have been discussed. At least senior management have talked to us.'

'I take it you mean Dr D'Angelo?'

Grace smiled. 'They certainly don't come any more senior.'

Beth frowned. 'I suppose he talked you into it?'

'Actually…' Grace grinned '…I suppose you could say he talked me *out* of it. I'd reached a point where I'd made up my mind to hand in my notice. Looking back on it, I realise it would have been a pretty stupid thing to do. He might have taken me at my word and, actually, I do enjoy my work.'

'Still, I can understand why you felt so unsettled. You've worked at The Hermitage for what? Five years? Six years? And most of those in a pretty senior capacity.'

'Six years. Mind you, sometimes it feels like for ever.'

'I know what you mean.' Beth sipped her fruit juice. 'Last time we spoke, you weren't too happy with the idea of having to uproot yourself and make a fresh start.'

'I will admit the idea didn't greatly appeal.'

'And now it does?'

'Well, it does put a different perspective on things, that I shall be going to the new clinic as Head of Department, with more responsibility and presumably more say in how things are run.'

'It sounds good.'

'I know.' Grace smiled over her glass. 'I almost cringe with embarrassment when I think how I stormed into Nick's office, fully prepared with a list of grievances and with my resignation already typed out. I can see now that it would have been a huge mistake. I made a lot of groundless assumptions as it turned out, most of them based on ignorance—and a touch of resentment that things weren't going to be done the way Max had always done them. I made some wrong assumptions about Nick himself, too.'

Beth's mouth tightened fractionally. 'I'm not so sure that the people who have been made redundant would share your renewed faith.'

'Yes, well, I admit there *have* been redundancies. But I know now that they were mainly staff who were due to retire anyway, and they've all gone with a more than generous pension, thanks to Nick. I know one or two members of staff have been offered employment in different departments, or at one of the other hospitals, and those who chose not to go have been compensated. But a few like myself have actually been promoted, so I have to say it hasn't turned out to be the disaster I imagined it might be.'

Beth picked up her fork and began to toy with her salad. 'It sounds as if he's done a remarkable sales job.'

'Oh, I don't think it was like that at all. I'm not

saying I don't think he could be ruthless if the need arose. But if I'm honest about it, I knew, and I'm sure most of the staff also knew, that things had to change.' She frowned. 'Max was a brilliant doctor and a good friend. But times change—medicine changes. I'm sure James must have guessed long before I did that things couldn't go on the way they were, but he was in a difficult position. He couldn't say anything, for fear of causing panic as much as anything.'

'So what you're saying is that it's the survival of the fittest.'

Grace shrugged. 'Whether we like it or not, private health care is big business. The sponsors have the finance and they know what it takes to succeed. You can't do that without a certain element of ruthlessness creeping in. It's a big, competitive world out there, Beth.'

Beth gave up all pretence at eating her food and pushed her plate away. 'And what about James? Where does he fit into the scheme of things?'

'Haven't you talked to him?'

'Not a lot. We both seem to have been busy.'

Grace frowned. 'To be honest, I can't say I'm surprised. No one seems to find it easy to talk to James these days. He's always in a foul mood but he won't discuss it. I know, I've tried. Still, I thought he might have talked to you.'

'Not so far. Not really, anyway.' She didn't want to think too much about her last conversation with James.

'I heard a rumour that he might be moving—somewhere up north.'

Beth felt her heart give a slight jolt. 'Really? I hadn't heard.'

'Well, there may be nothing in it. As I said, he isn't exactly talking to anyone these days, but I thought you might know.' She looked at her plate, pushing the pasta round with her fork. 'I don't think he and Nick exactly hit it off.'

Beth moistened her dry lips. 'Do you know why?'

Grace pulled a slight face. 'It happens sometimes, I suppose. A clash of personalities. But James is no fool. He must know if he chooses to go up against Nick he can't win. I just hope they can settle their differences, whatever they may be, otherwise, well, he may be better off elsewhere.'

Beth's startled gaze rose. 'You mean—with another company?'

'Or back in England. Why not? It may come to it. One thing's for sure,' Grace insisted, 'there's only one boss at The Hermitage, and that's Nick.'

'And you don't mind that?'

'No.' Grace reached for her glass and sat back. 'I realise now that he's fair, though not always sweet-tempered. In fact, I'll go so far as to say he's been like a bear with a sore head recently but, then, under the circumstances, I'd probably be the same.'

Colour darkened Beth's cheeks. 'What circumstances?'

'Well, I wouldn't like his responsibilities, would you? Apart from anything else, it must make for a pretty lonely life.'

Nick D'Angelo lonely? Beth felt her heart give a dull thud. 'I can't say that's the picture I get,' she said drily. 'I'm surprised he has time for empire-building.'

'You don't think the reports about his private life could be just a tad exaggerated? Besides, he's Italian, Beth.'

'Is that supposed to mean something?'

Grace shrugged, sitting back as the waiter brought their coffee. 'Their attitude towards their women is different. I mean, they all seem pretty laid back about most things—but when it comes to marriage it's a serious matter. You only have to see the Italians with their families to know that it's something special.'

Beth felt her hand shake as she stirred sugar into her coffee, wondering with a sudden sense of shock why it had never occurred to her before now that Nick might be engaged or even married.

She felt the colour drain from her face. 'Don't you think we might have heard if he was married?'

'You're probably right. I'd heard there was a girl... Mind you, I get the distinct feeling that he's the kind of man who likes to keep his private life strictly separate from his business. Who knows? Perhaps he finds it has certain advantages.'

Beth felt the breath snag in her throat. She pushed her cup away and forced a smile. 'This has been lovely, Grace. I hate to cut and run but I really have to get back.' She reached for her bag, but Grace waved away her attempt to take the bill.

'I'll get it. My treat. I'm glad we managed to get together. I didn't want to leave without saying goodbye, and thanks for all your support over the past few years. I wish you the best of luck, too. Things are going to change. It's probably going to mean a lot more hard work and extra responsibility, but I can't think of anyone better suited to it than you.'

'I hope you're right. I'm still not sure I'm up to it.'

'You'll be fine.'

They walked out of the café into the heat of the afternoon.

'I hope things go well for you as well.' Beth smiled. 'You deserve it. I expect I'll see you again before you leave.'

Driving back to the hospital, Beth found herself battling against a sudden crazy urge to burst into tears. Her hands clenched on the steering-wheel, and she drew a sharp breath, telling herself she was behaving like a fool. What Nick did with his private life was no concern of hers. Frustratingly, that didn't make it any easier to put the memory of that kiss out of her mind.

It was late afternoon by the time she escorted the last of her patients to the door.

'Give the anti-inflammatory tablets a try, Mr Henderson.' With an effort she forced a smile. 'And try not to do anything too strenuous for a few days.'

The man turned gingerly to look at her. 'I'll try, Doctor. It's not so easy, though, not when you're on holiday and the kids want to be kept entertained.' He gave a wry laugh. 'I thought I was going to end up spending the week in hospital when I woke up this morning and found I couldn't get out of bed because my back had seized up. Luckily the manager at the hotel suggested I come to the hospital. I'm glad now that I took his advice.'

'Yes, well, take it easy and you'll be fine. No more lifting heavy suitcases.'

'Don't worry. I've learned my lesson.' Dave Henderson waved and made his way slowly along the corridor.

Beth was sitting in the office, tapping notes onto her computer, when Jill returned to the office and collapsed into a chair.

'Phew! It's hot out there.' She fanned her cheeks with a piece of paper. 'I swear I'll never get used to it.'

Beth glanced up. 'How did it go?'

'You really want to know?' Jill eased off one sandal and massaged her foot. 'Which would you like first? The good news or the bad news?'

Beth gave the other woman a long, steady look then leaned forward to pour her a glass of cool mineral water. 'Here, you look as if you need this.'

'Oh, great. You're a lifesaver.' She took a long drink before pressing the cool glass to her cheek.

Sitting back, Beth carefully eased the panic from her voice. 'I think you'd better tell me what happened. Or did he refuse to see you?'

'Oh, no, he saw me.' Jill grinned. 'As a matter of fact, he was utterly charming. I explained the situation, that you had other commitments which couldn't be changed at short notice. He listened, and then he took me out for lunch. A working lunch,' she added quickly, 'which, under the circumstances, I thought was very nice of him.'

Beth gave a sigh of exasperation. 'But what about the report?'

'Oh, I gave it to him.'

'And?'

'Well, he accepted it.'

Beth ran a distracted hand through her hair. 'But did he say anything? I thought it was urgent. Didn't he say anything, express an opinion?'

Jill threw her a derisive look. 'Oh, come on, Beth. It was a pretty hefty report. You didn't expect him to sit there and read it there and then, surely?'

'No, of course not. Well, not to go through it in detail anyway.' Beth drummed her fingers impatiently on the desk. 'Didn't he at least glance through it, skim the last few pages? Express his satisfaction that I'd managed to complete it?'

'Er... Actually, no. He seemed more concerned about what we should eat. Sorry.'

Beth waited, battling against a rising sense of frustration. 'So, what did he do with it?'

Jill glanced at her and muttered something under her breath.

Beth frowned. 'I'm sorry, I didn't quite...'

'He sort of—well, he dropped it into the filing cabinet.'

'Dropped it. You mean, that was all? After all my hard work, racing to put ideas together? He didn't even comment?'

Jill looked at her. 'I rather suspect that anything he might have said would be unrepeatable.'

'You mean he was angry?'

'No, not angry. Just...sort of quiet, that's all.' She pulled a wry face. 'I'm not sure it was wise, me going in your place.'

Beth swallowed hard. 'You did explain that I already had a prior engagement, one I couldn't break at short notice, and that it might have been better if he had given me prior warning?'

'I said all of that, and more. Believe me, I went out of my way to grovel on your behalf.'

'And what did he say?'

'Not a lot.' Jill shot her a dubious look. 'He told me to say that when you're ready to talk, you'll know where to find him. Oh, and something about postponing the inevitable, but I didn't quite catch that. Sorry. I was too busy thinking that if I'd known I was going to be taken out to lunch by a gorgeous hunk, I'd have worn my new dress. Anyway, what will you do?'

What she wanted to do, Beth thought, was to pretend that none of this had happened, that she had never been kissed by him, that she had never even met Nick D'Angelo.

She took a deep breath and reached for the phone. 'I'll call him.'

'I wouldn't bother right now.'

'I don't really have a choice, do I? Not if I want to get the extra equipment and new facilities we all know we need—*he* knows we need.'

'I hear what you're saying, but he said he'd be unavailable for the rest of the day, due to other commitments.'

He was playing her at her own game, Beth thought, except that, as far as she was concerned, it wasn't a game. With a sigh of exasperation she put down the receiver and rose to her feet. She moved to the window, a slim figure in the calf-length skirt and sleeveless blouse she was wearing. 'You say he took you to lunch?'

'It seemed like a good opportunity to put your case

to him, so I accepted his invitation,' Jill said lightly. 'I enjoyed it. We got on surprisingly well. He talked about some of his own ideas for expanding the work of the hospital. He's really keen to open the facilities up to local non-paying patients, and he talked about taking on more spinal injury cases. At the moment most of them have to be taken to the main hospital in town, which can be quite a trip by ambulance for a seriously injured patient. He thinks we could take on more responsibility, provided we update our theatre facilities.'

'He obviously made a deep impression on you,' Beth said tightly.

'Oh, I don't think he was trying to impress me. What he said made sense. I mean, we all remember that awful coach crash last year, when two holidaymakers were killed and about eight other passengers were seriously injured. We could only take two. The rest had to go to the main hospital.' Jill frowned. 'He wants to improve things around here and, heaven knows, there's plenty of scope for improvement. Give him some credit, Beth.'

Jill's enthusiasm seemed to engender a deep resentment in Beth, which she knew to be unreasonable.

'It's all very well coming up with the ideas, but these things don't come cheaply. Extra operating facilities require extra trained, highly specialised nurses.'

'I pointed that out, but he didn't seem too concerned. I got the impression he can handle the sponsors.'

'I'll bet he can. It'll be interesting to find out how many of them are female.'

Jill threw her a look of exasperation and rose to her feet. 'Oh, well, at least I tried.' She paused at the door. 'You know what I think?'

'No. But I'm sure you're going to tell me.'

'I think you're scared.'

Beth turned to look at her and gave a slight laugh. 'I don't know what you mean.'

'I think you do,' the other girl said softly. 'I think you're scared because you've actually discovered that you like the man and he makes no secret of the fact that he likes you, and you don't know how to deal with it.'

'Aren't you jumping to some rather groundless conclusions?'

'Am I? Beth, I don't know what's happening between the two of you, but he's right—you can't avoid him for ever.'

Beth drew a ragged breath. 'I've no intention of being just a name on his list of conquests, thank you very much.'

Jill smiled wryly. 'You've been listening to gossip, and I think you're being unfair. You only have to look at him, Beth, to know he doesn't need to chase women. They're practically lining up. He could take his pick and frankly I could be tempted to join the queue.'

'What exactly are you trying to say?'

'I think you're in love with the man,' Jill said softly. 'You just don't want to admit it, even to yourself.' She opened the door. 'Anyway, don't forget to phone him. You may not like the idea but he's still the boss. I'm just going off duty, but I'll be in tomorrow if you need to make any changes to the report.'

'Fine. I've some paperwork to do then I'm off, too.' Beth glanced at her watch. Suddenly she felt exhausted. 'Actually, I may take my copy of the report home with me and take another look at the figures. Some things I may be able to compromise on if it comes to it. Some I'm not. It's probably as well if I have all the facts and figures firmly fixed in my head.'

In fact, she thought as she drove through the traffic later, she welcomed anything which would take her mind, even briefly, off a seemingly ever-increasing awareness of Nick D'Angelo and his looming presence in her life.

CHAPTER SEVEN

THE day's heat had lessened slightly by the time Beth let herself into her apartment, and she immediately set about flinging open the windows to let in a welcome breeze.

A sudden feeling of exhaustion seemed to come over her and she decided to take a shower, changing into a cool cotton nightie and a silk wrap before making herself a cup of coffee and a sandwich.

Two hours later, she knew that she couldn't put off the final moment of contact any longer. She had picked up the phone so many times, only to replace the receiver, that when she finally forced herself to dial Nick's number her hand was shaking with tension.

Even now some part of her hoped that he would be out, so that when he answered tersely at the first ring, it needed every ounce of will-power not to slam the phone down again.

He had obviously been sitting by the phone. Waiting for her call? Beth moistened her lips nervously.

'Nick, this is Beth. I hope I didn't disturb you.'

There was a moment's hesitation before he answered, 'It's late. I imagined you must have gone to bed by now.'

She pushed a hand through her hair. 'It's not that late. Anyway, I've been working. I had some paperwork to do. I've been busy.'

'So I gather. I hope you enjoyed your lunch.'

'Yes, thank you. As a matter of fact, I did.' She twisted the flex of the phone in a nervous gesture between her fingers. 'That's why I called.'

'To tell me how much you enjoyed your lunch?'

'No.' She stiffened defensively at the edge of sarcasm in his voice. 'That wasn't what I meant at all. I...I rang to explain why I couldn't meet you today.'

'You don't have to make excuses. Your secretary already spoke nobly in your defence. I trust you'll see that she is suitably rewarded for her loyalty.'

'They weren't excuses,' Beth snapped. 'Jill was telling the truth. I had a prior engagement which I couldn't...wasn't prepared to break simply in order to fit in with what was a purely arbitrary arrangement on your part. Perhaps if you'd given me more notice...'

'There's nothing in the least arbitrary about a contract, Beth.'

'I hardly think it gives you the right to behave unreasonably.'

There was a fractional pause. In the fleeting seconds of silence, she wished she could see his expression, then was glad she couldn't as he drawled softly, 'Still fighting, Beth?'

She drew a shaky breath. 'I'm simply trying to explain.'

'That you think I was being unreasonable.'

'Yes. No...' He was doing it again, confusing her.

'I made you a promise, Beth. Business is business. Pleasure is something else, which needs its own time and place. I don't confuse the two.'

'And is that what you think I'm doing?'

'Isn't it?'

'I don't see it that way.'

'No.'

She drew a deep controlling breath. 'No.'

He said softly, 'You've been avoiding me. I'm glad. It means I was right. You do care and you're afraid I'll prove it to you.'

Her mouth tightened as she sensed that he was deliberately provoking her into an argument she would never win. 'Why don't we talk about the report?'

'What *about* the report?'

'Look, can we stop playing games?' she said flatly. 'You said it was important that I should come up with ideas and make a strong case. I spent hours working out figures. So when do you wish to see me? Or perhaps you're not really interested. Perhaps you have your own agenda.'

'I don't work that way, Beth. The fact is, we had an appointment several hours ago, which *you* failed to keep.'

'I have explained,' she said impatiently. 'Look, I have my diary here now.' She reached for it, flipping the pages. 'Give me a date and a time. I'm sure we can come to some new arrangement. How about tomorrow? Or the day after?'

'I'm sorry but that won't be possible. In any case, I'm not in the habit of rescheduling appointments once they're made.' His voice opened up a chasm between them.

'So what do you want me to do?'

'I think you know what I want, *cara*.'

She flushed, sensing his quiet laughter. 'I was talking about the report. I thought the figures I came up with were reasonable. I know the new hydrotherapy pool would be expensive, but—'

'When I've read it and come up with some conclusions, I'll be in touch.'

'Yes, but—'

'You'll hear from me, Beth. But right now it isn't convenient. I'm expecting an important call.'

Her mouth twisted. 'From a female, no doubt.'

'As a matter of fact, yes. What's the matter, Beth? Surely you can't be jealous?'

She drew in a sharp breath, wondering why the cool admission should shake her.

'Why, you...' She heard Nick's quiet laughter and it was several seconds before she realised the phone had gone dead. Shaking with anger, she replaced the receiver. He was paying her back, of course. Making her wait, knowing what the uncertainty would do to her. But as for being jealous, the very idea was ludicrous. Or, at least, only days ago that would have been true.

She was still staring at the phone when the doorbell rang, and she blinked hard, dashing a hand against her eyes. She certainly wasn't expecting anyone. Tying the belt of her robe more securely around her waist, she went to open the door.

'James! What on earth are you doing here—at this hour?'

He looked at his watch. 'It's not very late, is it?'

It is when you've had a bad day, she thought.

He stood, frowning uncertainly at her. 'Look, I know I should have phoned first, but I had an emergency admission at the hospital, an appendicitis case, so I was late getting away. I had to see you.' His gaze went past her. 'This isn't a bad time, is it? You're not…?'

'I don't have a visitor, James, if that's what you're trying to say.' She held the door wider. 'You'd better come in. Unless you feel that you being here at this time of night might be misinterpreted.'

'I'm sorry.' He had the grace to flush. 'I suppose I deserved that.'

'Oh, I'd say so.' She moved away, switching on a small lamp, purposely not asking him to sit. 'It's a little late for a social call, isn't it?' She hadn't intended the contempt in her voice to sound quite so obvious, but it found its mark.

He stood uncertainly, clearly discomfited by her coolness. 'You're right. To be honest, it's taken me a while to pluck up the courage.'

Beth frowned. 'To do what?'

'To say I'm sorry.' He gave her a direct look. 'I know I can't take back the things I said—they were out of order. But I want you to know that I realise now that I might have jumped to a few conclusions.'

'Only a few!' She looked at him, trying to sympathise with the uneasy figure he made. 'Am I to take it that you realise they were unfounded?'

He shrugged. 'I had no right to pass judgement.'

'Too right you didn't, so why do I get the impression that's precisely what you're still doing?'

His mouth tightened. 'Damn it! You're not making this easy, Beth.'

'Good. I'm glad to hear it. What exactly is it that you're trying to say?'

'I just…I just wanted you to know that I realise I had no claim on you. I've always thought—well, we work together, and I've always thought we were friends, but what you choose to do with your private life is up to you. It's none of my business.'

'I see,' she said with restrained anger. 'So, in other words, you haven't come here to apologise. You're actually saying that you're generously prepared to turn a blind eye to my…misguided indiscretions? Is that it?' She faced him, bristling with anger now. 'James, I think you should leave, right now. There's clearly nothing more we have to say to each other.'

James stood his ground. 'Come on, Beth,' he responded. 'That's not what I said.'

'Oh, really? Well, in that case, you're obviously not saying it loudly or clearly enough.'

He dug his hands in his pockets. 'That's probably because I'm not finding this easy. Beth, I came to say that I'm leaving and, whether you believe it or not, I shall miss you. I see now that I made a mistake in coming, but I didn't want to go without saying goodbye, that's all.'

Her face paled. 'You're leaving? James, you're not…?'

'No,' he said quickly. 'I'm not being dismissed or sent up north after all. It seems that my talents can be used elsewhere. Apparently there's a new surgical unit opening up in one of our larger sister clinics in Spain. They think I can do the job. I don't know what—or who—persuaded them to take me on, but I'm grateful. I've always preferred surgery.'

'Yes, I know.'

'There hasn't been much opportunity at The Hermitage—at least, not as much as I would have liked. As you know, most major cases have usually gone to the main hospital. I know this move will be quite a challenge, but actually, I have to admit, I like the idea of a new start, a fresh challenge.'

'But that's marvellous.' Her thoughts flew to Nick, and her colour deepened as she remembered the exchange they had had on this very subject. 'I'm so pleased for you. I'm really glad things have worked out.'

'I'm glad, too.' When James took her in his arms, she offered no resistance. 'As a matter of fact, I was rather hoping you might consider coming with me. You're a good doctor, Beth. I'm sure a place could be found on the new team. It could still work, you know? Between us, I mean. It must at least be worth a try.'

'I don't think so, James,' she said awkwardly. 'Too much water has gone under the bridge. We're good friends. I hope we always will be. That means a lot to me.'

'To me, too. But I'd thought...hoped it would become something more than just friendship. You must have realised that.'

She shook her head, detaching herself gently from his arms. 'I'm sorry, James, I really am, but I can't honestly say I thought of it in that way. I'd always assumed, naïvely I suppose, that marriage required a certain element of trust.'

'Hell!' His mouth twisted. 'I guess I deserve that.'

'No.' She shook her head. 'I'm sorry. But it wouldn't work, you know.'

'It's D'Angelo, isn't it?'

Her eyes darkened. 'Not the way you think.'

He studied her pale face. 'He's got to you, hasn't

he? Beth, I just don't want you to get hurt, that's all. His sort make up their own rules as they go along.'

Her breath snagged in her throat. 'I appreciate your concern, really.'

'It's more than that,' he said softly. His hands applied gentle pressure on her arms. 'If ever you need a friend, someone to talk to…'

'You'll have to write and let me have your new address, tell me what the new unit is like.' She wished he would leave. Most of all she hoped he wouldn't kiss her, forcing her to make comparisons.

'There's still time to change your mind and come with me. I'd wait.'

'It's a nice thought, but it wouldn't work.' With an effort she managed to smile. 'You've got a whole new future ahead of you, doing something you've always wanted to do, and I have a contract here.'

'Contracts can be broken.'

She flushed. 'Not this one. I've made a commitment and I'll see it through. Besides, you don't need—'

'Don't say it.' His fingers brushed gently against her lips. 'As for the bright new future—well, that remains to be seen.'

She smiled. 'You'll be fine, James. You're a good doctor. You'll be doing a job you love.'

'But I won't have you with me.'

She looked up at him and kissed him gently on the cheek. 'You don't need me.'

There was a long pause and then he said huskily, 'Ever since we met I've known you were something special.' He rushed on without giving her a chance to speak. 'I just want you to be happy, that's all.' Then he said, in an attempt at lightness, 'Anyway, I'd better go. It's getting late and I have some packing to organise.' His hands rested briefly on her shoulders. 'So this is goodbye, Beth. I wish you luck.'

'You, too, James.'

She watched him walk away and toyed briefly with the idea of calling him back. But it was no use. She didn't love James. She loved Nick, but there was no future in that. No future at all.

CHAPTER EIGHT

IN THE space of a week, the temperature had, if anything, risen even higher. The Italians thrived on it. Geraniums in the window-boxes which festooned every house and café thrived on it. Even after several years in the country, Beth still found herself wondering if she would ever become properly acclimatised.

She walked into the office, set her briefcase down and promptly sank into a chair and lifted the heavy swathe of honey-blonde hair from her neck.

'Phew! It must be ninety degrees out there already, and the day's hardly started yet.'

Jill grinned as she flipped the switch on the electric kettle which she kept in the office, precisely for times when she needed to get on undisturbed. 'Coffee?'

'Oh, yes. Thanks. You're an angel.'

'You know your trouble? You're used to too much cold British rain.'

'You could be right. I'd welcome a short, sharp shower of rain right now. Mmm, lovely.' She stirred sugar into the cup of coffee Jill placed before her on the desk before sitting back, glancing over the list of messages Jill had strategically placed before her on the blotting pad. 'So, what have we got here, then?'

'Just a few things that need your attention before you head off to Accident and Emergency.'

'The latest lab report on little Adam Bates.' Beth scanned the page and gave a nod of satisfaction. 'This is much better. His chest is clear. His temperature has been normal for the past forty-eight hours. I reckon we can give the all-clear for him to go home.'

'His mum will be pleased.'

'I'm sure she will. It's been a worrying time for her, and not much of a holiday either. Still, I'll be seeing them this morning so at least I can give her some good news for a change.'

Jill handed her a buff folder. 'I gather Alice Craig is going home tomorrow.'

'Yes. I'm really pleased with her. She's made good progress and I know Ted will keep a firm eye on her—see that she sticks to her diet and takes the right amount of exercise. It makes so much difference when a patient has good support from relatives.'

'I think he'd do anything just to have her home again. These letters just need your signature, by the way, then I'll get them in the post later today. Oh, yes, and there's an invitation to attend a conference next week. Food and wine will be served. Strictly informal.'

'And a medical sales rep behind every potted palm, order book at the ready. I don't think so.' Smiling, Beth reached for her pen and wrote, 'No—make excuses.' 'Is that it?'

'I think so, for now anyway, but the day is young yet. Right, well, I'll start working my way through the latest mountain of paperwork, then.'

And nothing from Nick. In a week, not as much as a phone call, no sign of him anywhere. If he had deliberately made up his mind to avoid her, he was doing a good job.

Beth rose restlessly to her feet, pushing her chair

back and crossing to the window to look out on the busy street. She had spent the last few nights tossing and turning, trying to imagine going back to England, making a fresh start, building a new life for herself—only to be haunted by the realisation that it would be a life devoid of the one thing she really wanted.

She went to her consulting room, telling herself resolutely that she would put Nick firmly to the back of her mind. Except that it was easier said than done when the mere thought of him seemed to exert a depressing power over her ragged emotions.

Her hand hovered uncertainly over the phone. Where was Nick? More to the point, who was he with? Beth was shocked by the sudden pang of jealousy which tore through her like a physical pain. If nothing else, this past week had given her an insight into what it would be like not to have him around, and she didn't like what she saw. Professionally she would survive, but on a personal level? From the moment Nick had walked into her life, the edges of her reasoning had become blurred. Her life had been uncomplicated. All neatly mapped out. Now it was anything but.

The trouble was that she had kept her emotions in cold storage for so long, imagining they were safe. What she hadn't bargained on was someone like Nick D'Angelo coming along and rekindling the fires, and the trouble with fire was that you could get more than your fingers burned. But, then, she wasn't a child any more, she was an adult, and she could see the dangers.

She had just begun to tap out his number when Maggie tapped at the door and walked in.

'Hi. Sorry, I didn't mean to interrupt, but I think we need you in A and E.'

'That's all right.' Beth was conscious of the tiny feeling of disappointment that swept through her as she dropped the receiver back in its rest. 'I was just about to come over there anyway.' She shrugged herself into her white coat. 'What's the problem?'

'Well, we had a chap admitted about...' Maggie consulted her notes '...a couple of hours ago. I gather he works on one of the cruise-ships. Anyway, he was brought ashore when the ship docked earlier today because he'd been complaining of feeling unwell and the ship's doctor wasn't too happy about keeping him on board. He thought the man's symptoms needed further investigation.'

Beth frowned and matched her footsteps to her friend's as they hurried along the corridor. 'And what do we know about him so far?'

'Not a great deal. He seems to have a fluctuating temperature. At first we thought it might be a straightforward dose of flu, but now we're not so sure.' Maggie frowned. 'We've been tepid-sponging and monitoring him since he was admitted, but there doesn't seem to be any improvement—in fact, I'd say he's gone downhill slightly in the past hour, so I thought I'd better get you to take a look at him.' She led the way through the swing door. 'We've put him in the side ward, just as a precaution.'

'Good thinking,' Beth said reassuringly. 'Even if it is flu, we don't really want to spread it around if we can avoid it.' She uncoiled a stethoscope from her pocket. 'Right, let's take a look at him. By the way, what's his name?'

'Raju Patel. Apparently he's been working for the shipping company as a cabin steward for the past two years.'

'Right. And do we know anything about his previous medical history?'

'Nothing untoward, apparently.'

'OK. Let's take a look at him.'

Maggie nodded, standing aside to let Beth precede her into the small side ward.

Raju Patel was about twenty-five. He lay huddled beneath a blanket, his eyes closed. He was shivering violently, despite the day's heat.

'Hmm. I see what you mean. He's not looking too good, is he?' Beth leaned forward. 'Mr Patel, can you hear me? I'm Dr Bryant. I gather you're not feeling too well.'

The man groaned, but didn't open his eyes.

'I think that's all the response you're going to get. We've all tried talking to him.'

Beth straightened up. 'When did you last check his temperature?'

Maggie consulted her notes. 'A quarter of an hour ago. It was just over forty degrees.'

'Well, I suppose it's possible it *could* be flu. Has he complained of a headache at all?'

'Apparently, a couple of days ago, and of feeling shivery.'

'Any other pain?'

'Sorry, we haven't been able to get any more information out of him.'

Beth drew the covers back and gently but firmly palpated the man's abdomen. She frowned. 'Any vomiting?'

'Not that we know of. Certainly not since he was admitted.'

'OK. Let's have a listen to his chest. It's possible there could be an infection lurking.'

Seconds later, she straightened up, shaking her head. 'Well, his chest is quite clear.'

'So where do we go from here?'

'First of all, we keep him isolated, at least until we know what we're dealing with. We're going to need a blood film.'

'I've already seen to that,' said Maggie. 'It went down to the lab, and I've stressed that it's urgent.'

'Good for you.'

'You're not convinced it's flu, are you?'

'No, I can't say I am.'

'Could it be some sort of viral infection?'

'It's possible but, again, I don't think so. Has anyone else on board the ship presented with the same symptoms?'

'Not so far.'

'In that case, I'd lay odds it isn't viral.' She frowned. 'There's evidence of enlargement of the spleen.'

'So what do you reckon?'

'I think we could be looking at malaria. It's not something I've come across before, but it's on the increase, unfortunately.' She consulted the man's notes. 'I see he spent his last leave at home in India, visiting his family, which might explain it. Even if he's still taking his regular antimalarial drugs, it can still happen.'

'Right. So, how do you want to proceed?'

'We'll start him on a combination of chloroquine

and primaquine. He'll need daily blood tests, and we need to watch carefully for any signs of renal or respiratory involvement.'

'I'm glad I called you,' Maggie said as they walked towards the work station. 'He's not going to be too happy about the ship leaving without him.'

Beth gave a wry smile. 'Right now I think he's past caring. Anyway, he can fly out and rejoin them later.' She wrote up her notes and handed them over. 'There you go. I'll come in and take a look at him later.' She glanced at her watch. 'I have a phone call to make. See you later.'

'*Ciao.*'

Back in her own room, Beth paced restlessly to the window, conscious of a tight knot of tension in her stomach. Sooner or later, she knew, she had to talk to Nick, and the only reason she was putting it off was because then she would have to admit to herself what it was that she was really feeling. The question was, did he want to hear? It seemed he had spent the past week avoiding her. Playing her at her own game, maybe? Making her wait, knowing that, sooner or later, she would have no choice but to come to him.

She drew herself up sharply. This line of thought wasn't getting her anywhere. He was right, they had to talk. Even so, the thought sent a quick shaft of panic running through her as she returned to the desk, reached for the phone and briskly dialled his number.

Within seconds a voice answered. 'Medics International. Can I help you?'

'Yes.' Beth forced herself to take several deep, even breaths. 'I wish to speak to Dr D'Angelo.'

There was a muffled pause at the other end of the

phone, as if the speaker had covered the receiver. Beth waited, tapping her pen on the desk.

'Hello, caller. I'll put you through to the medical director's personal secretary.'

'But I don't wish to speak to his personal secretary,' Beth snapped. 'I need to speak to Dr D'Angelo—in person.' She swallowed hard. 'Tell him it's Dr Bryant. Beth Bryant.'

'I'm sorry, Dr Bryant, but all Dr D'Angelo's calls are being directed through his secretary right now.'

'But this is urgent—and personal,' she ground out. 'I'm calling from the hospital.'

'I do understand, Dr Bryant.' An audible sigh accompanied the words. 'I'm putting you through now.'

Beth's hand shook then tightened as a different but unmistakably female voice came on the line.

'*Pronto*. May I help you?' the Italian-accented voice asked.

Beth closed her eyes briefly. Her own voice sounded unnatural, trapped in her throat. 'I've already explained that I need to speak to Dr D'Angelo—in person.'

'*Si*, Dottore Bryant.' The voice was soothing and infinitely patient. 'I do understand. Unfortunately, I'm afraid the director isn't available. This is Carla Falco, his personal secretary, speaking.'

Beth's lips tightened as if to stifle the protest that was welling up inside her. Not again! It couldn't be happening again. 'Perhaps you can tell me when he *will* be available?'

'I'm very sorry, Dottore Bryant. Right now I really can't say. I'm afraid he is away.'

Beth's heart lurched painfully in her breast.

'But...surely you must have some idea as to when he's due back?'

'I'm sorry, no, I haven't. He left rather suddenly, and his plans are a little uncertain.'

Beth bit at her lower lip. 'Yes, I see, but I need to speak to him on an urgent matter. I have a report—'

'I don't think you should worry about it, Dottore Bryant. I understand that in his absence everything connected with the modernisation project is being handled by our head office in Rome.'

'Rome!'

'*Si*. I understand that the company's sponsors are holding a meeting there. As a matter of fact, I received a fax from Dottore D'Angelo earlier today, instructing me to book you on the earliest possible train. I was going to phone you with the details later, when I had confirmed them.'

Taking a deep breath, Beth sat down. 'They want me to go to Rome?'

'Yes, I know.' Carla sounded vaguely troubled. 'It is rather short notice, but I have managed to make arrangements for you to travel the day after tomorrow, and I understand that you'll be meeting our major sponsor, Dottore Andretti, who will discuss the project with you, and you will be able to put your ideas to him then. I'm afraid I can't confirm the precise time of that meeting, but you will be given more information when you arrive in Rome. A hotel reservation has also been made for you.' There was a momentary pause. 'I hope this isn't going to be awkward for you. You can make the journey? Only I believe there is some question of urgency.'

Foraging amongst the papers on her desk for her

diary, Beth fought for self-control. Pencilling quickly through the appointments already listed there, she scrawled a quick note. 'I'm sure I can arrange for a colleague to cover for me for a couple of days. I take it it will only be a brief stay?'

'Oh, I imagine you can safely make that assumption, *Dottore*. The date on the return ticket has been left open. I'll have the ticket, and your hotel reservation details sent round to you by special courier.'

'You appear to have thought of everything,' Beth said drily.

'I'm afraid I can't take credit for that. Dottore D'Angelo thought of everything. I'm simply carrying out his instructions.'

'I see.' Beth's mouth twisted. 'And in the event that I might not have...found it convenient, I suppose there was some contingency plan?'

There was a slight pause before the woman laughed. 'Do you know, I don't believe it even occurred to him. How like a man!'

How like this particular man, Beth thought. She was surprised to find that her hand was shaking as she replaced the receiver. The one consoling thought in the whole affair was that, temporarily at least, she had gained another breathing space. Yet somehow even that thought failed to offer the comfort she had hoped for since, though in reality he might be far away, in her dreams there were no barriers and no defence. He had said she couldn't run away for ever. Her lips quirked. But at least this time she would have a head start!

CHAPTER NINE

ROME was hot and noisy, and full of tourists. To Beth, seated in the car which had met her at the station, there was something exhilarating about it all as she sat back, feasting her eyes on the sprawling, tireless city.

The colourful awnings of roadside cafés flapped gently in a desultory breeze. The small, flower-filled squares were filled with businessmen and pretty girls drinking coffee.

Beth fanned her cheeks, finding almost no relief, despite the car's open windows. What she wanted more than anything right now was a long, cool shower and a glass of iced coffee—not necessarily in that order.

The driver glanced in his rear-view mirror and smiled. 'This is your first visit to Rome? *Si?* You are here on holiday?'

Beth met his gaze and smiled wryly. 'No, I'm afraid not. I've been to Rome several times and I love it. But this time I'm here on business.'

'Oh, this is a pity. Rome is a good place.' He grinned, showing even, white teeth. 'Especially for lovers.'

'Yes, I'm sure it is. Sadly I'm not going to have time for sightseeing. I have to work.'

He frowned. 'You take time. Is not right to come

to Rome and not enjoy. I show you all the best places.'

Beth sat back against the upholstery. 'You work for Medics International, don't you?'

'*Si.* Yes, sometimes.' He smiled. 'But you want to see the sights. I show you.' He reached into the glove compartment and handed a card over his shoulder. 'Here, you take this. You want to see real Rome, not where the tourists go, you call me. Ask for Roberto.'

Smiling, Beth tucked the card in her bag, knowing she would never use it. But still, she thought as she stared out of the open window, there was nothing to prevent her coming back some day. Except that, as Roberto had said, Rome was a place for lovers.

She straightened her shoulders, clamping down forcibly on her thoughts, unaware that a pair of dark eyes watched and wondered what could possibly have caused the faint flush that suddenly darkened the girl's pretty features.

Roberto looked at his watch. 'Hotel is not far now. Is very nice—you like.' He indicated ahead as the car turned a corner.

The square was lined by large, exclusive hotels, cafés and tall office buildings. Palm trees grew alongside orange trees. The car turned yet another corner and slid to a halt. 'Hotel Trevi.' Roberto leapt out to open the car door for her. 'I bring your bags.'

'That's all right. I only have the one. I can manage.' She stood on the pavement as he got back into the car and waved.

'OK, don't forget—you call, anytime.'

She paused on the steps, briefly appreciating the

modern building before making her way into the cool airiness of the hotel's reception area.

A girl, pretty, dark-haired, wearing a cool T-shirt and knee-length skirt, smiled as Beth approached her.

'*Buongiorno, Signora.*'

'*Buongiorno.*' Beth put her bag down. 'I have a reservation. The booking was made through Medics International. The name is Bryant, Dr Bryant.'

'Oh, yes. Dr Bryant. Welcome to Rome. You are expected.' She pressed a bell located on the desk. 'We have a suite already prepared for you.'

'A suite?' Beth frowned. 'I think there must be a mistake. I don't need a suite. A room will be fine. I really don't expect to be here for long.'

The girl reached for her register again in obvious confusion. 'No, there is no mistake. A suite was reserved.'

Beth frowned, then shrugged. 'Oh, well, I expect it's just a mistake. I'm sure it can be rectified in the morning.'

The receptionist smiled. 'I'll have someone take your luggage.' She glanced at the solitary bag. 'The rest is in the car?'

'No, I have only one bag.'

The girl seemed momentarily taken aback. 'Yes, of course, Dr Bryant.' She reached for a key. 'The suite is yours for as long as you wish it and, of course, the hotel's facilities are entirely at your disposal.'

Beth smiled. 'It's a nice thought. Unfortunately I doubt if I shall have time to take advantage of them. I'm here on business.' She paused. 'I believe I'm supposed to meet with a Dr…Dr Andretti. Perhaps you can tell me if the appointment has been arranged?'

The girl flipped through the pages of a large register. 'Ah, yes. It is here. For ten o'clock tomorrow morning. You know where the offices of Medics International are?'

'No, but I have the address. I'll take a taxi. Thank you.'

Beth followed a porter who led her from the lift to her suite, where he unlocked the door and stood back to allow her to enter.

She did so, making no attempt to conceal a gasp of delight as she walked into the room, fragrant with the perfume of flowers. From the sitting room, complete with easy chairs and a writing desk, she wandered through to the modern bathroom and a bedroom furnished in cool, neutral tones.

So much luxury, she thought wryly, and so little time to enjoy it. It was all a far cry from her own small apartment. Running a hand experimentally over the large, king-sized bed, she banished a fleeting but infinitely disturbing thought that it would make a delightful honeymoon suite.

Breathing hard, she closed the door firmly behind the porter and went straight to the bathroom to douse her burning cheeks with cold water. As far as she and Nick were concerned, the honeymoon was over even before it had begun. But she was appalled to discover the effect that even the mere thought of him had on her. He might be a long way away, and for the first time since he had walked into her life she should have felt safe. But somehow safe didn't quite equate with happy.

Next morning, Beth stood at the window of the modern office block, gazing down at the street below. The sun was hot and people were already bustling to and fro like an army of ants, she thought.

She had been escorted to the conference room by one of the staff who had explained that Dr Andretti would be with her shortly, and could she get Beth some coffee while she waited?

'No, thank you. I'll be fine.' Besides, her stomach was already fluttering nervously, without the added stimulus of caffeine.

Glancing at her watch, she forced herself to sit in the chair and reached into her briefcase for her copy of the report. She didn't need to read it. She had gone over and over the figures until her head ached. But knowing them and persuading a man she had never met that The Hermitage was worth a large investment of cash... She tried not to think about the alternative. The threat of possible closure made her nervous to the point where her hands were actually shaking.

Rising to her feet again, she pushed the weight of her hair from her face, already conscious of the slight beading of perspiration on her back due to nerves. Five more minutes and she would pick up the phone on the desk and ask if she had been forgotten.

She looked at her watch again. Ten-thirty. So much for the corridors of power! She should have had that coffee after all. She had felt too restless to eat breakfast. Instead, she had taken a long, cool shower, leaving her damp hair to hang loosely about her shoulders as she had dried herself and slipped into pastel-coloured undies and a sleeveless, scoop-necked dress of cool linen.

Just for a second, catching a glimpse of herself in

a large mirror, Beth wondered whether she should have chosen to wear something more formal. The pale ivory dress, although simple, seemed to emphasise the colour of her eyes, while the neat waist and straight skirt accentuated her slim figure.

But, then, its suitability or otherwise was hardly relevant, she thought, turning away from her reflection, since it was too late to do anything about it now.

She tapped the fingers of her right hand against her wrist and was about to look at her watch again when the door opened and she turned to greet Phillipe Andretti. Dry-mouthed, she had actually managed to force her lips into a smile of greeting before her panicked gaze flew to the tall figure who stood motionless, watching the look of disbelief on her face as his eyes raked over her.

'Aren't you at least going to say you're pleased to see me, *cara*?'

Stunned into shocked immobility, she was scarcely aware that he took the hand she still held outstretched, pressing his lips gently to her fingers as the all too disturbingly familiar voice mocked her.

She stared at him blankly, telling herself it was all a dream, then felt the colour burn slowly into her cheeks, knowing, alas, that it certainly was no dream. Nick D'Angelo was devastatingly real. 'You!'

For a few seconds she stood in numbed disbelief before sanity returned. Without even giving herself time to think, she had wrenched her hand from his grasp, gathered up her briefcase and was heading for the door.

She had actually made it when his hand suddenly

gripped her arm, and she was swung round to find herself looking up into Nick's strong features.

'Beth, wait,' he said softly as she struggled in his grasp.

'I don't believe this is happening.' Her eyes blurred, and she took a deep breath before trying to pull herself angrily from his grasp. 'Is this some kind of joke? Let me go.'

'We need to talk. I can explain.'

'Somehow I doubt that.' Her eyes flashed stormily as he held her. 'In any case, I don't want to hear anything you have to say.'

But he didn't let her go. Instead, he pushed the door quietly closed behind her, and with cool deliberation drew her towards him. 'I'll let you go when you've calmed down and listened to what I have to say.'

She fumed inwardly, fighting a battle she knew she couldn't win as his grasp merely tightened. She pushed against him, tried to put some distance between them as she became frustratingly aware that, in spite of herself, her body was responding to his nearness.

'This isn't what you're thinking, Beth.'

'You don't know what I'm thinking.'

'Maybe not,' he said thickly, 'but I can make a pretty good guess. And I don't blame you. It probably does look bad.'

She gave a short laugh. 'Oh, I'd say so. I think you planned this. I'm only surprised that I was naïve enough to fall for it.'

'You have to believe me. It wasn't planned, Beth. I didn't want it to happen, not like this.'

She told herself she had to stay calm and felt her

heart thud as she stared into the dark, sombre eyes. 'I...I want to believe you, but how can I?'

His glittering eyes looked down into hers, and she saw them widen briefly before he drew her roughly into his arms. 'God, I want you,' he said raggedly. 'I told myself. I swore I wouldn't let this happen, but it seems I only have to be near you...' For a second he looked at her, then she felt the strength of his powerfully muscular body against hers as his mouth came down in a kiss that was soft and melting. She felt as if she was merging with him, making her a part of him. His hands were gentle and caressing. He stroked her hair, her cheek.

'I didn't plan this,' he said again, his voice muffled against her hair.

At first she tried to resist him, her eyes closing as a feeling of weakness washed over her. This wasn't supposed to be happening, but her responses seemed to be coming from somewhere totally beyond her control.

'Beth, have you any idea how I feel?' he groaned huskily. 'Tell me you're glad to see me.'

The spell was broken. With a soft cry of protest she wrenched herself out of his arms. Her hand went out guardedly as he moved towards her. 'Don't!' She was all too aware of the effect he was having on her emotions.

'I swear, it wasn't planned.'

'Then you'll be able to explain all of this,' she said drily, the sweep of her hand encompassing the conference room. 'Explain the hotel suite, the car, my travel arrangements. Explain all of that, and tell me why I'm here. Better still, tell me why *you* are here when I was told I was to meet Dr Andretti.'

'None of this means you were lied to, Beth.'

She gave a short laugh. 'You'll forgive me if I find that difficult to believe.'

'I can understand your anger.'

'Oh, good. Well, that's all right, then.'

He frowned. 'Beth, Phillippe Andretti is my grandfather.'

For some reason she couldn't even begin to explain, she felt a sensation of relief sweep over her. 'Y-your grandfather?'

He stood, watching the varying emotions racing over her face. 'We both know I didn't have to bring you here in order to make love to you,' he said softly.

The cool confidence in his eyes made her pulses race.

His expression was unreadable. 'My grandfather still wants to see you, Beth.'

'I'm not at all sure I still want to see him.' A frown momentarily etched its way into her forehead. 'What could I possibly have to say to him?'

'What do you want to say?'

'I was under the impression that I was here to deliver a report which might have some impact on the future of the hospital—one way or another.' She licked her dry lips. 'Or shall I assume that the decision to close has already been taken?'

'There has been no decision. I value your opinion. I've always known that we could work together. In spite of our...differences, we share the same aims. You're a good doctor. I've seen your work. I trust your judgement.'

'Y-you do?' She laughed shakily. 'I don't know what to say.'

'We both want what's best for the hospital.'

She eyed him warily. 'So why am I here?'

'Because my grandfather is the chief sponsor, and he asked to see you.'

'You mean I need to win his approval, too.'

The dark eyes narrowed enigmatically. 'Something like that.'

'I see.' She frowned. 'In other words, I'm on trial. Damn it, Nick! You have no right to do this to me. Give me one good reason why I shouldn't walk out of here right now. You can keep your contract—and the job. I don't need it. I really don't care.'

His hand caught her wrist as she made for the door. 'I can't let you do that, Beth.'

'It isn't your decision. I won't play your games.'

'Beth, my grandfather had a heart attack just over a week ago. That's the only reason he isn't here.'

She stopped struggling, staring at him as his words slowly began to register. A week ago. So he hadn't been avoiding her. She had misjudged him. 'Oh, no! I'm so sorry. I don't know what to say.' She swallowed hard. 'H-how is he?'

'He's fighting back, because that's the sort of man he is.'

'Was it bad?'

'Bad enough. When my sister called to tell me, it was very much touch and go.'

She frowned, trying to take it all in. 'But he will be all right. I...I know how much he means to you.'

'The danger period has passed, but you'll understand that I want to see him again.'

She looked up at him, seeing the lines of weariness etched into his face. 'But surely he can't still want to see me?'

'He still has his faculties, Beth. He may be old, he may be ill, but he's still head of the family and we respect him.'

She straightened her shoulders and nodded. 'I'll be ready whenever you want to leave. I only need to pack my overnight bag. Just let me know.'

'I'd like to leave first thing in the morning.'

She nodded again, pausing in the open doorway. He had already turned away and was standing with his hands in his pockets, staring out of the window. 'I...I really am sorry, Nick.'

He shrugged without turning to look at her. 'So am I, Beth,' he said softly. 'So am I.'

It was only as she hurried back to her hotel to begin repacking her bag that it occurred to her to wonder if they had both been talking about the same thing!

They left early next morning. The sun was already hot as the car sped along the roads into the Umbrian countryside, and Beth was glad she had chosen to wear a thin, silky blouse with her cotton skirt. Even so, she shifted uncomfortably as a tiny rivulet of sweat ran down her back.

'Why don't you relax, make yourself more comfortable?' Nick took his eyes momentarily from the road to look down at her. 'Go to sleep if you want to. I'm not one of those drivers who need constant conversation.'

Glancing from beneath her lashes at the firm profile, Beth tried to decide whether he meant he *pre-*

ferred silence. Personally she found it unnerving, or perhaps that was just down to his close proximity. The small sports car didn't allow for much distance between driver and passenger.

Flushing slightly, she rested her head back and closed her eyes, not to sleep but with the deliberate intention of trying to shut him out of her thoughts.

Some time later, he manoeuvred around a tight bend. Caught unawares, she slid towards him, her body making solid contact with the muscular hardness of his thigh.

Straightening up quickly, she pulled herself away, her throat tightening as the scent of the aftershave he was wearing evoked memories she would far rather had lain dormant.

'Sorry.' She sat back, bracing herself in her seat.

His mouth tightened briefly. 'Go back to sleep. You must be tired.'

'It must be the heat.' And the fact that she hadn't got much sleep last night! 'I didn't mean to drop off like that. I thought I'd only closed my eyes for a few seconds.'

'You slept for nearly an hour, Beth.'

'Oh.' Her eyes met his, and there was a slight movement at the corners of his mouth.

'Don't worry about it. I can drive quite safely with your head resting against my shoulder. You aren't exactly heavy.'

She turned away quickly, staring in confusion at the scenery which, she knew already, would stay imprinted in her mind for ever. Even the light seemed different as the sun rose in the sky, its heat hanging over the green hillsides. It was so breath-takingly beautiful.

Nick's voice cut across her thoughts, and she had to blink hard before she could force herself to look at him.

'Sorry, did you say something?' For a brief moment she wondered what had caused the slight tightening of his mouth before he shook his head.

'It wasn't important.' He glanced at his watch. 'We're almost there. You'll be able to relax soon.'

Was her state of tension so apparent? she wondered.

Almost as he said it, it seemed, the car turned in through the gates of a large villa and slid to a halt on the drive. Beth had barely time to catch a glimpse of the flower-strewn walls before Nick was climbing out of the car and holding her door open. For a moment she hung back, suddenly reluctant to intrude. So this was his home. Beth was conscious of a nagging ache deep within herself, a feeling she decided it was safer not to pursue.

'Are you going to get out?' His voice came down to her. 'Or do you plan on sitting there until it's time to leave?'

Scarlet-cheeked, she scrambled out, only to find that, instead of moving, he had reached out a lazy arm, trapping her against the car.

'I just want you to know that I'm not giving up on you, Beth.'

Something about the way he said it sent a sudden tremor running down her spine. Reassurance? Or a threat? Her startled gaze flew up to meet his, but the question was never asked as a tall, slender figure came running down the steps towards them and, without as much as a glance in Beth's direction, flung herself into Nick's eagerly waiting arms.

Beth had to look away as jealousy seared through her with the heat and intensity of a forest fire, its violence threatening to choke her.

CHAPTER TEN

BETH stood motionless, waiting for the two to break apart and remember her presence, and in the interlude found herself staring in rapt fascination at the girl from whom Nick was now gently but unhurriedly detaching himself.

Feeling her breath snag in her throat, Beth had to admit that she was lovely. Evenly tanned, slender, with dark hair, the girl was beautiful and typically Italian. It might have been easier if she could have found something to dislike, she told herself, but there was nothing as the brown eyes looked perceptively in her direction.

'And this must be Beth.' The girl smiled and murmured something softly in Italian. It had sounded friendly enough but, whatever it was, Beth was surprised by the sudden ominous tightening of Nick's features as he reached into the car for her bag.

'We're both hot and tired, Lucia. How is Grandfather?'

'He is sleeping peacefully. He seems a little better today. Piero is sitting with him.' She led Beth up the stone steps into the cool, tiled interior of the villa, frowning slightly. 'Piero sends his apologies. He is looking forward to meeting you, but later perhaps after you have rested. We all eat together.'

Beth threw a confused glance at Nick. 'Piero?'

'Piero is married to my cousin, Lucia,' Nick

drawled softly. 'Did I forget to tell you?' Mocking laughter lurked in his eyes.

Beth managed a tight-lipped smile. 'You may have done. I really can't remember.' The sudden contact of his hand on her arm sent a tiny quiver of excitement running through her, but she managed to detach herself from his grasp and smile at Lucia. 'As a matter of fact, I'm not tired at all, just rather hot and thirsty.'

'I have refreshments prepared. Some fresh lemonade or iced coffee, perhaps? Or would you prefer tea?'

'Lemonade sounds marvellous.'

Lucia smiled. 'Come, then. Out here you will be cool.' She led them out to a terrace which overlooked a garden and a small vineyard, and Beth couldn't contain a quiet gasp of pleasure.

Lucia left them for a few moments, returning with a tray of glasses and a jug which she deposited on the table. 'Please…' She looked shyly at Beth. 'While you are here, you must think of this as your own home. I know Nick will wish it.'

Beth blushed. 'That's very kind of you but—'

'There is a pool. I swim every morning when I'm here.' It was Nick who poured the drinks and handed her a glass.

'This is true,' Lucia confirmed wryly. 'Sometimes I think he never sleeps.'

Beth stolidly refused to meet his gaze. 'I never have that trouble myself, but that's possibly because I have a clear conscience.'

She heard the rasp of what may have been laughter in his throat.

'I find waking early has its advantages. You should try it.'

She swirled her drink furiously, clinking the ice against the glass. 'I'd hate to spoil your routine.'

'But it's not my routine that's in danger, Beth.' The softly spoken words were barely audible, but her heart suddenly started beating in an erratic fashion. Rising briskly to her feet, she set her glass on the tray.

'If you don't mind, I would rather like to go to my room and freshen up.' She spoke deliberately to Lucia, and had to bite back a sigh of frustration as Nick immediately rose to his feet.

'Good idea,' he said. 'I could do with a cold shower myself right now.'

Afraid—or unwilling—to interpret the glint in his eyes, Beth purposely turned her back on him to follow Lucia, telling herself she hadn't heard the whispered 'Coward' or his following laughter.

Lucia opened a door and Beth followed her into a bedroom. 'I hope you will be comfortable. If there is anything you wish, you must say.'

'Oh, no, it's beautiful. I'm sure I have everything I need.' A carefully arranged vase of flowers had been placed on a table beside the bed, but it was the bed itself which drew her attention, and warm colour suffused her cheeks as Nick came slowly towards her. Her breathing quickened. 'I thought you wanted to take a cold shower.'

His strong gaze swept her face. 'Not wanted, Beth, *needed*. There is a subtle difference.'

Lucia stood in the open doorway, her gaze flitting uncertainly from one to the other. 'I will leave you to unpack. I must go to Grandfather. It is time for his medication.'

'Please, don't worry. I can manage.' She looked determinedly at Nick, and drew a panic-filled breath as he made no attempt to leave. He was the most powerfully sexual man she had ever known, and she had never been more physically aware of him than at that precise moment.

She closed her eyes tightly, knowing that if he were to kiss her now she wouldn't be able to resist him. She felt his hand brush gently against her cheek, the curve of her throat. But the kiss didn't come.

Her eyes flew open to meet his, then moved away again as she realised he was frowning. She stood frozen, unable to move. She *wanted* him to kiss her. She broke away and took a deep breath as she saw the look of taut strain on his features—as if he knew precisely what she had been thinking.

Her stunned gaze followed him to the door, and it was only the sudden realisation that he was leaving that gave her back her voice.

'Nick, I... Where are you going?'

He looked suddenly impatient. 'I really do need that shower.'

'Yes, but...'

A muscle tightened in his jaw. 'My room is only next door, Beth. If you need me, you have only to call.' He turned smartly on his heel and walked away, leaving Beth feeling as if she had been struck by lightning. For several minutes after he had gone, she sat on the huge bed, shaking. Then the thought hit her like a huge tidal wave. She wanted Nick in her life. This was where she wanted to be. She was filled with a need to be part of him.

Shocked by the admission, she pressed a trembling hand to her mouth. In spite of all the self-made promises, somehow it had happened. All the time she had been afraid to fall in love, and the irony now was that the only man ever to break through her defences had made it perfectly clear that it wasn't *love* he wanted!

Beth took her time over her unpacking, and waited until there was no sound from the adjoining room and she was sure Nick must have gone downstairs before she finally risked opening the door.

A shower had gone some way towards reviving her physically, and by the time she had slipped into clean undies, cotton trousers and a shirt which she knotted at the waist, she was feeling slightly more human as she went downstairs and out to the terrace.

Having steeled herself to see Nick, it came as a relief to find Lucia sitting alone. She had obviously been for a swim. Her hair was sleeked damply back, and she had pulled a short robe on over her bikini.

She smiled shyly as Beth joined her. 'I thought you might want to sleep. In Italy everyone takes a siesta until the sun is less hot.'

'I can't say I blame them.' Grinning, Beth lowered herself into one of the loungers.

'I'm afraid Piero has had to leave. He was sorry not to see you, but tonight at dinner you will definitely meet.'

'I look forward to it.' The more the merrier, Beth thought. 'What does your husband do?'

'Oh, he is a doctor in the city, but while Grandfather is so ill he has been coming home to spend some time with him.' She rose to her feet. 'You haven't eaten. There is some salad and fruit.'

'No, really, I'm still not very hungry, just thirsty.'

'There is iced coffee in the jug, but I can always get something else.'

'No, please,' Beth protested. 'The coffee looks delicious.' She sipped at the long glass Lucia handed her and nodded her approval.

'Perhaps you would like to sit in the shade.'

'I suppose it might be wiser.' Beth smiled wryly. 'I'm always advising my patients not to overdo the sunbathing.' Her eyes took in the profusion of trailing colours which adorned the walls and terracotta tubs as Lucia led her up an external staircase and into a drawing room.

'You have a beautiful home.'

'Not mine—Nick's.' Lucia smiled. 'Although he seldom comes here now.'

Beth looked at her in some confusion. 'Oh, I had no idea. I'm sorry, obviously I misunderstood.'

'You didn't know.' Lucia sent her a slanting glance. 'Nick bought the villa some years ago.'

'I see. I suppose his work means that he doesn't have time to come here as often as he would wish. He must miss it.' How could anyone not? she thought wistfully.

'I suppose in time he may wish to come back,' Lucia said. 'For now, he is happy that his grandfather can be here.' She smiled sadly. 'The old man is very strong-willed in spite of his years. He was determined they would not take him to the hospital. And who knows? Perhaps he was right. He would not have wished to be with strangers.' Her hand rose. 'In any event, Nick would never have allowed it to happen.'

'I can understand why he is so worried.'

Lucia nodded. 'They have always been close. Nick is sitting with him now. Sometimes I think he feels he must make the most of the time they may have left.'

Beth toyed with her glass, conscious of a slight feeling of guilt that they should be discussing Nick in his absence. 'His grandfather must be an exceptional man to have raised a small child more or less single-handed.'

'Nick has talked to you about himself?' Lucia eyed her perceptively.

'Oh, no, not really, only that his parents died when he was still very young and that his grandparents raised him.'

'Then he has told you more than most.'

Beth frowned. 'He doesn't strike me as the sort of man who exchanges confidences easily.'

'He is a very private person. He chooses to hide his feelings. In many ways he and his grandfather are very much alike.'

'You mean they are both stubborn?' Beth couldn't resist.

Lucia laughed softly and, rising from her chair, crossed to the bookshelf. 'That, and in looks also.' Returning to where Beth sat, she handed her an open snapshot album. 'You can see the resemblance here, very early on. Nick was no more than ten when this picture was taken, but already the likeness is there.'

Gazing at the picture of a young boy standing on

a beach beside an older man, Beth felt her throat tighten. 'Yes, I see what you mean.'

'They were always together. They shared everything, the good times and the bad.'

Beth turned the pages, conscious of a feeling almost of intrusion, and yet she felt compelled to go on, to experience this part of his life she had never dared hope to see. 'He must have missed his parents dreadfully.'

'Their deaths hit him very hard.'

Beth's hand shook as she turned the page. They were the sort of pictures one would find in any family album, yet for some reason her eyes filled with tears.

She had to blink hard as she came to another photograph of Nick, again with his grandfather, but now they were older and this time there was a girl, a lovely girl with long, black hair, shading her eyes from the sun as she smiled directly into the camera. Nick's arm was draped lazily, yet almost possessively around her bare shoulders, and something in his expression as he gazed down at her sent a pang of sheer jealousy searing through Beth.

She glanced up at Lucia and, almost as if anticipating the question, an odd expression crossed the girl's face. 'That is Claudia. She is beautiful, is she not?'

Beth swallowed the sudden painful tightness in her throat. 'Yes, she is. Very beautiful.'

Lucia suddenly closed the book, returning it to the shelf. 'Of course, no one was surprised when Nick announced that he had asked her to be his wife.'

Beth felt the colour drain from her face. 'His... Nick has a wife?'

'She was just twenty when they married. There was such a celebration. It seemed to go on for days.' She broke off. 'Are you all right?'

Beth nodded. Lucia's voice seemed to be coming from somewhere far away. She rose shakily to her feet. 'Yes, thank you, I'm fine. You were telling me about the wedding.'

'Ah, yes. The celebrations. It was all such a happy time. Who could have guessed that a year later she would die.' Lucia stopped suddenly, a look of dismay filling her eyes. 'But I thought you knew this.'

'No, I...' Beth closed her eyes, trying desperately to shut out a horrifying vision of the pain he must have suffered. If only she had known, could have guessed!

'What...what happened?' She saw the brief flicker of hesitation in the girl's eyes. 'I need to know. It is important.'

'It was a car. The road was very narrow.' Lucia's eyes were suddenly very bright. 'She was on her way to meet Nick. A child ran into the road. She swerved. Another car was coming towards her. It was already too late. She was dead before anyone could reach her.' She looked at Beth. 'I was so sure Nick must have told you.'

'I suppose there was no reason for him to have done so. I only work for him, you know.'

Lucia looked perceptively at her, and for a moment her brow furrowed. 'I think perhaps Nick has learned to hide his feelings too well.'

'But why would he wish to hide them from me?'

'Perhaps even more so from you.' Lucia spoke the words with a sudden measure of shyness. 'It might be easier if he felt nothing for you, because then he would have no fear of being hurt.' She looked directly at Beth. 'You love him, I think.'

Beth licked her dry lips before saying bleakly, 'Yes. Very much.'

'Then you should not worry. Whatever troubles there are between you can be swept away.'

'I'm not sure it's that simple.'

'Sometimes pain can become a habit, a cloak almost, to conceal what is real and may be dangerous. Nick is not a coward. Perhaps he also needs to be sure of your feelings for him before he can make himself vulnerable again.'

Beth nodded slowly, and in an impulsive gesture she went to hug the girl.

'I hope you're right.'

'About what?'

Nick's voice, coming quietly from behind her, brought the colour rushing into her cheeks, and she turned swiftly to face him.

'Secrets, Beth?' He raised dark eyebrows and Beth was grateful for the normality in Lucia's voice as she answered for her.

'It is women's talk. Not for your ears.'

His face seemed suddenly drawn and suddenly gaunt as he looked at Beth. 'My grandfather has asked to see you, but don't stay too long,' he warned. 'He likes to talk, but he still tires very easily.'

'Don't worry,' she said evenly. 'I won't encourage him.'

'It's a pity you can't offer some guarantee of immunity to the rest of us,' he ground out savagely. Before she could even begin to give voice to a stunned protest he was striding away, leaving her to gaze in anguish after his fast-retreating figure.

Entering the room in answer to a quiet summons, Beth found herself hesitating as her shocked gaze registered not the product of her imaginings but a head of snow-white hair and a face in which, despite all the evidence of his illness, the eyes still remained acutely alert and mobile.

'Signora Bryant. Beth. Please, come closer so that I can see you more easily. My eyes are not what they were.' His voice beckoned and Beth went towards the chair where he sat by an open window, feeling a spasm of compassion tighten her throat as he held out his hands. She placed her own in them and smiled. Phillipe Andretti, in his eightieth year, was still a striking figure of a man.

'Forgive me for not greeting you upon your arrival.' He indicated a chair. 'Please, sit beside me. I would get up, but Lucia would only start fussing and my grandson would feel obliged to tell me I should know better.'

The gentle humour behind his eyes sent a dull ache through Beth as she began to understand something of the closeness between this man and Nick. Lucia had been right, Beth thought. Despite the distance of years, they were alike.

She smiled. 'They love you very much. I'm sure they only want what is best for you.'

He waved a hand deprecatingly. 'Tender plants are to be cosseted, not old men.' He leaned forward, the action causing a spasm of coughing and breathlessness. Beth half rose to her feet in concern, clenching her fingers against the impulse to reach out and check his pulse.

'You're tired. Perhaps this is not a good time. You should get some sleep. I can always come back later.'

Phillipe Andretti chuckled, waving her back to her seat. 'What I would like is a glass of good red wine, but my grandson prefers to listen to my old mule of a doctor who is even older than I and who never enjoyed the taste of good liquor in his life.'

In spite of herself, Beth laughed. 'I'm sure he only does what is best for you. Can I get you something else? A glass of orange juice, or some iced water perhaps?'

He gave a snort of impatience. 'Even my taste for wine is not what it was.' He sat back, studying her face. 'I am tired. Talk to me. Tell me about yourself.'

'There isn't a great deal to tell. I'm sure you'd find it very boring.'

He laughed and there was a frailty in the sound which alarmed her. 'At my age, when every minute is precious, even to be bored is a blessing. But I think you are unkind to yourself, my dear.'

She swallowed hard. 'What would you like to hear?'

'Whatever you wish to tell me,' he said softly. 'I would not wish to intrude.'

But that was precisely what he was doing, Beth thought, battling with a momentary flicker of irritation, which was instantly replaced by one of guilt, and she felt herself blush. 'I wasn't thinking of it as an intrusion. It's simply that, compared to what you have here, where everything is so beautiful, my life in a small apartment must seem rather uninteresting.'

'Do you find it so?'

She met his shrewd gaze and smiled. 'No, as a matter of fact, I don't. I love my work. I love Italy, and at the end of a hard day, especially when things may not have gone quite as I would have hoped, there is something very reassuring about being able to close my door on the world.'

'I think you will not be alone in thinking so.' He smiled before the dark gaze settled again on her face. 'You live alone?'

'Yes. It may seem old-fashioned by today's standards...'

'Not by my standards.' Phillipe Andretti smiled. 'All women secretly wish for a man to protect them, is this not so? Even when it is only from their own foolishness.' He leaned forward and smiled. 'My grandson is right, you *are* beautiful. All the more reason you should have the protection of a strong man.'

Beth gave a slight laugh. 'I don't think—'

'It shocks you that my grandson finds you beautiful?'

'No! At least... No, not exactly.'

'Then perhaps you are offended that he talks to me of his feelings.'

'I think you may have misunderstood his feelings.'

A frail hand came to rest over her own. 'Tell me, Beth,' he said quietly, 'why are you here?'

'Because...because I was told you wished to see me to discuss the hospital. I understood you wanted to approve the new ideas.'

'Ah!' He nodded. 'My grandson told you this?'

Beth swallowed hard. 'I understood that your approval was necessary.'

An odd expression crossed the old man's face. 'My grandson is in many ways more traditional than even he would choose to admit.'

Beth frowned. 'I don't understand. What has his being traditional got to do with any of this?'

'Perhaps more than even I had realised,' he said softly. 'There is only one reason why Nick would wish for my approval. Only once before he asked it, when he brought to me the girl he wished to marry.' His hand tightened over Beth's. 'I began to think he would never find happiness again. He does not need my blessing, but I give it gladly.'

Beth stared at him. 'No, I don't think you understand. Nick doesn't want to marry me. He doesn't love me.'

Phillipe touched her cheek, and suddenly she realised that he was gently wiping away tears. 'Did Nick tell you this?'

She shook her head. 'He doesn't need to say it.'

He gave her a quick look which was almost arrogant in its disapproval. 'You know my grandson so well that you can read his mind—better than I who raised him?'

She drew a ragged breath. 'I know he loved Claudia.' She heard the old man's sharp intake of breath. 'What he feels for me could never compare. I couldn't take her place, and I wouldn't presume to try.'

'Tell me, little one, do you love my grandson?'

She drew a deep, shuddering breath. 'Yes.'

'Then why have you so little faith in him?' He shook his head. 'I know there has been tragedy in your own life.'

'Y-you know?'

'Nick tells me those things which are closest to his heart, and he speaks of you. If you, in spite of everything, have found room in your heart for my grandson, then why is it so difficult to believe that he can do the same?'

Beth shook her head and rose slowly to her feet. 'Because it isn't the same.' She turned to look at him. 'I had stopped loving my husband even before he died. Oh, I didn't want it to happen. I tried to stop it happening.'

'Some things are not for us to decide.'

'But don't you see?' Beth sighed. 'Nick still loves Claudia, and I don't think I can bear it.' Without a backward glance she ran from the room, still blinded by tears, so that she was barely aware of the grim-faced figure who stood there or who called her name.

Within the safety of her own room, Beth flung herself onto the bed and wept in earnest, deep, painful sobs which racked her body with such intensity that she wasn't even aware of the door opening until a hand brushed the hair from her cheek. She raised startled eyes to gaze into Nick's gaunt face.

For a moment she lay staring at him through a blur of tears, telling herself that he couldn't possibly be there, any more than she could be seeing the expression in his dark, pain-filled eyes. Then he was beside her, gathering her in his arms, his weight above her as he kissed her with an urgency that was both gentle and relentless.

'Beth. Oh, Beth!' he moaned savagely as his lips burned over her mouth, against her hair, his hands cupping her face as he forced her to look at him. 'For God's sake, don't cry. I can't bear it.'

She wasn't even certain why she was crying, except that she loved him, and now he was actually with her it no longer seemed to matter that he didn't want her love. In one blinding flash of realisation she knew she would settle for what he was prepared to give, even though some day it must end. For now, it was enough that he was here and that she loved him. Later—much later—she would think about losing him.

Without thinking, she arched herself against him, returning his kiss, and for one moment she felt his body tense above hers.

'Nick, make love to me,' she murmured, her hands feverishly tugging aside the barrier of clothing between them. She sensed rather than saw the shock widening his eyes as he stared down at her, restraining her hands.

'Beth, for pity's sake, do you know what you're doing? Lord knows, I want you,' he said huskily, 'but you'd better be warned. I don't think I'm going to be able to stop if you change your mind.'

As if in answer, her hands continued to make a gentle, still nervous exploration of his body. 'I won't change my mind.' Her hands cupped his face, forcing him to look at her. She could feel the heat of his skin against her own, the taut arousal of his body, which said more clearly than words how much he wanted her.

'Beth, are you very, very sure?' He lifted his head and she silenced his words with her fingers.

'Make love to me. The reasons don't matter.' Her

hands stroked his shoulders, the nails digging into the muscular flesh, and she felt him shudder uncontrollably as she deliberately continued the movement along his spine.

'Oh, God...' His voice was muffled against her throat, and suddenly she knew that, in spite of his physical male strength, at this moment he was the more vulnerable of them.

His voice was hoarse as he drew her towards him, caressing her body, moulding her to him until it seemed they became one, and in the moment of possession her swift cry of pleasure brought his mouth back to hers.

For a long time she lay in his arms, exhausted yet exhilarated. It was only when she turned to look at Nick, thinking he must have fallen asleep, that she realised, blushing, that he was studying her, the dark eyes glittering as they roamed every centimetre of her body, and she felt herself shiver with excitement as he turned towards her again.

'You're going to have to explain, Beth,' he breathed. 'I've wanted you too long, had you fight me...'

'Are you saying that you have regrets for what just happened?' A tiny flicker of fear widened her eyes, and she heard him swear softly.

'Right now I just need to know that you aren't going to disappear, like some beautiful dream, the minute I let you go.' His eyes darkened. 'If I thought that might happen, I'd never let you go, Beth,' he rasped.

'I won't disappear,' she told him huskily. 'I realised suddenly that you were right when you said I couldn't run away for ever, that I had to face reality.' She swallowed hard as tears threatened to well up in her eyes.

For a long moment he looked down at her, before sliding down beside her. 'I said a lot of things,' he muttered against her hair as he kissed her with surprising restraint. 'Things I had no right to say.'

She put her arms out, drawing his head towards her breast. 'But you were right. I just didn't want to admit it. I was so scared of having it happen all over again, don't you see? I told myself I wasn't going to be hurt a second time.'

'And you thought *I* would hurt you? Is that what you're saying?'

'I couldn't take the risk.'

'What did he do to you, Beth?' he demanded softly. 'What sort of hold could he have had that made you even think you could sacrifice the rest of your life to the memory of a dead man?'

She tried to turn her face away as humiliation washed over her like a huge, suffocating wave, but he wouldn't let her.

'Tell me, Beth. Lay his ghost to rest once and for all.'

She drew a long breath. 'Paul's death was my fault.'

He frowned. 'That's crazy,' he said tersely. 'How could you possibly be to blame?'

She had to force herself to look at him. 'Perhaps not directly, but maybe I could have done something—*should* have done something—to prevent it.'

'How the hell could you have done that?'

'I don't know,' she protested, feeling her eyes fill

with tears. 'Perhaps...if I'd loved him more...h-he might not have started to drink.'

Nick's mouth tightened grimly. 'He was drunk? Did he hurt you?'

She had to look away from him now. 'It all happened so gradually. At first he just started to lose his temper.' Her mouth quivered. 'I think he began to resent me, even the fact that I gave up my chance of promotion so that he could get the senior job.' She shuddered. 'One day he actually hit me. The day he died, he had been drinking. Oh, he denied it, he always did, but by then I knew all the signs, and anyway I could smell it on him.' She gave a brittle laugh. 'In some ways, he was so naïve. He really imagined I couldn't tell. Or...or perhaps he stopped caring.'

She frowned and was silent for a moment. 'I hid the car keys to stop him taking the car. It didn't fool him. He guessed what I'd done and started demanding them, and when I refused to hand them over, he knocked me to the floor.'

Nick swore softly. 'Go on.'

'I don't think he meant it,' she said quickly. 'I just don't think he knew his own strength. Anyway, I must have been stunned for a few seconds, but it was enough. By the time I could try to stop him it was too late. He had found my handbag, tipped the contents out and taken the keys.' She moistened her dry lips with her tongue. 'He didn't get more than half a mile. The police came to tell me. They were very kind and understanding, they said he died instantly. The car went off the road, into a ditch.'

She was sobbing quietly, and with a curse Nick took her in his arms. He lay with her body pressed against him, hugging her close, rocking her gently. 'I'm sorry, Beth. I should have understood.' He lowered his face to kiss her, smoothing the hair from her damp cheek, and she saw his eyes widen as if in some dawning realisation. 'Is that why you don't drink alcohol?'

'I can't.' Her throat tightened. 'It makes me sick.'

He groaned softly. 'But why do you blame yourself for what happened? You couldn't stop him drinking. Even his resentment of you wasn't logical.'

'But don't you see? Perhaps if I'd done something different…'

'It wasn't your fault that he destroyed whatever there might have been between you, Beth. You have to face the fact that some people are weak. What *we* have is good and real.'

And it would have to be enough. It *would* be enough, she told herself, for as long as it lasted. And when it was over she would have her memories. It seemed her life was full of them.

'Beth, what is it?' Forcing her to look at him, Nick was shocked by the misery in her eyes.

'I know…about Claudia.'

She waited for the anger to darken his face. Instead, he bent his head to kiss her mouth.

'I know. Lucia confessed in a state of panic that she had told you, imagining that you already knew.'

'But…don't you mind?'

'Why should I mind you knowing, Beth? True, I loved Claudia. She was beautiful and gentle, and the brief time we had together was…' he drew a ragged breath '…was so perfect I didn't think I'd ever be able to face the rest of my life without her.'

Beth's fingers closed convulsively against his skin. She wanted to cry as a tight ball of pain filled her chest. 'I know...I know I can never take her place, but it doesn't matter. You were right. What we have is good, and it's real,' her voice rasped thickly, 'and it's time I faced reality again. I want to face it with you. I don't even care how long it lasts, a day, a week...'

Suddenly he had tensed above her, and Beth shivered beneath the brilliant fury in his eyes. 'What the hell are you trying to say?' His hands tightened on her shoulders so that she flinched with pain.

She swallowed convulsively. 'I just want you to know that I don't mind. That I'll be whatever you want, for as long as you want.'

With a husky oath his mouth closed over hers in a kiss that seemed to burn itself not only on to her lips but into her soul as well. She gave a soft whimper of protest as he broke away for a few seconds to look down at her.

'I want you for as long as there is, for the rest of my life and beyond. I want everything there is of you and more. I love you, Beth.' He ran his hands over her body, stroking, seducing. 'I intend to prove it to you now but, I warn you, there's no escape.' He lifted her up to meet him and her arms went round his neck.

'No more barriers, Beth?'

'No more barriers,' she promised, offering her own proof in the only way she knew how.

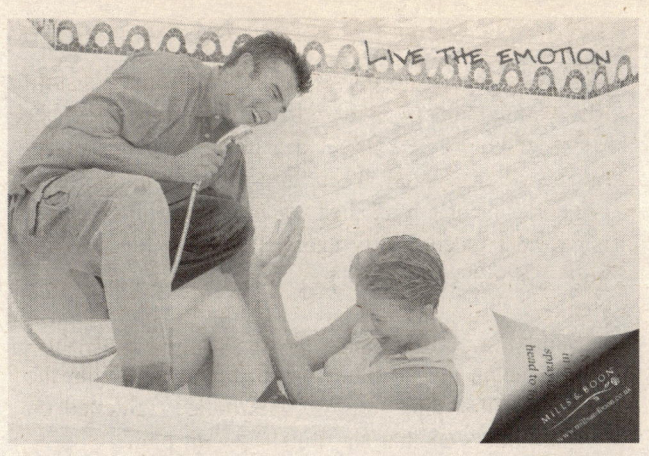

LIVE THE EMOTION

Modern Romance™
...seduction and
passion guaranteed

Tender Romance™
...love affairs that
last a lifetime

Medical Romance™
...medical drama
on the pulse

Historical Romance™
...rich, vivid and
passionate

Sensual Romance™
...sassy, sexy and
seductive

Blaze Romance™
...the temperature's
rising

27 new titles every month.

Live the emotion

MILLS & BOON®

MILLS & BOON

Live the emotion

Medical Romance™

STORMBOUND SURGEON by Marion Lennox

Joss Braden is bored. In fact he's out of Iluka as fast as his sports car can take him! But the bridge is down — there's no way on or off the headland. Suddenly Joss is responsible for a whole town's health, with only Amy Freye's nursing home as a makeshift hospital — and the chemistry between Joss and Amy is incredible!

OUTBACK SURGEON by Leah Martyn

Gorgeous Nick Tonnelli isn't just a high-flying surgeon, he's also a Sydney socialite. Outback GP Abbey Jones is charmed but confused when he makes his interest clear. The attraction between them is overwhelming, but will the glamorous surgeon really want a relationship with her?

THE DOCTOR'S ENGAGEMENT WISH
by Gill Sanderson

Erin Hunter had been the most beautiful girl at school — and like all the boys Josh Harrison had been in love with her. Now they have been reunited, while working as GPs, and Josh finds his attraction to Erin as strong as ever. But Erin isn't as carefree as he remembers, and he is determined to discover what has changed her...

On sale 4th July 2003

Available at most branches of WH Smith, Tesco, Martins, Borders, Eason, Sainsbury's and all good paperback bookshops.

MILLS & BOON®

Live the emotion

Medical Romance™

DR SOTIRIS'S WOMAN by Margaret Barker

Dr Francesca Metcalfe is the most gorgeous woman Dr Sotiris Popadopoulos has ever seen, and while they are working together on Ceres Island he hopes they will get to know each other better. But it seems that Francesca has chosen her career over having a family, and Sotiris has his young son who is need of a mother...

HER SPECIAL CHILD by Kate Hardy

One look at locum GP Tina Lawson and Dr Alex Bowen is smitten — surely she must feel the same? She certainly does — but she can't risk getting involved with Alex. Her son Josh needs all her love and attention. But Alex is determined to prove passion will last — and two is better than one when it comes to caring for such a special little boy.

EMERGENCY AT VALLEY HOSPITAL
by Joanna Neil

Mistaking consultant Jake Balfour for a patient is bad enough — and if only he weren't so attractive... When Carys's sister is injured Jake's support is unexpected — but ever since her troubled childhood Carys has sworn off men. Could Jake be the man to change her mind?

On sale 4th July 2003

Available at most branches of WH Smith, Tesco, Martins, Borders, Eason, Sainsbury's and all good paperback bookshops.

MILLS & BOON®

Live the emotion

Coming soon

PENNINGTON
Summer of the Storm

The first in a new 12 book series from bestselling author Catherine George. PENNINGTON is a charming English country town—but what secrets lie beneath?

Available from 4th July 2003

Available at most branches of WH Smith, Tesco, Martins, Borders, Eason, Sainsbury's, and most good paperback bookshops.

MILLS & BOON

Medical Romance™

...catch the fever

We're on the lookout for fresh talent!

Think you have what it takes to write a novel?

Then this is your chance!

Can you:

- ✸ Create heroes and heroines who are dedicated, attractive, up-to-the-minute medical professionals who would move a mountain to save a life or resolve a medical case?

- ✸ Create highly contemporary medical communities and settings – city and country hospitals, GP practices, A&E Depts, Special Care Baby Units, IVF clinics, Emergency Response Units, midwifery, paediatrics, maternity, etc?

- ✸ Create fast-paced medical drama – think ER, Casualty, Holby City, Peak Practice, etc.

- ✸ Develop deeply emotional stories, ranging from the tender to the passionate, of medical professionals falling in love amidst the pulse-raising drama of their everyday lives?

If so, we want to hear from you!

Visit www.millsandboon.co.uk for editorial guidelines.

Submit the first three chapters and synopsis to:
Harlequin Mills & Boon Editorial Department,
Eton House, 18-24 Paradise Road,
Richmond, Surrey, TW9 1SR,
United Kingdom.

FREE
4 BOOKS
AND A SURPRISE GIFT!

We would like to take this opportunity to thank you for reading this Mills & Boon® book by offering you the chance to take FOUR more specially selected titles from the Medical Romance™ series absolutely FREE! We're also making this offer to introduce you to the benefits of the Reader Service™ —

- ★ FREE home delivery
- ★ FREE monthly Newsletter
- ★ FREE gifts and competitions
- ★ Exclusive Reader Service discount
- ★ Books available before they're in the shops

Accepting these FREE books and gift places you under no obligation to buy; you may cancel at any time, even after receiving your free shipment. Simply complete your details below and return the entire page to the address below. *You don't even need a stamp!*

YES! Please send me 4 free Medical Romance books and a surprise gift. I understand that unless you hear from me, I will receive 6 superb new titles every month for just £2.60 each, postage and packing free. I am under no obligation to purchase any books and may cancel my subscription at any time. The free books and gift will be mine to keep in any case.

M3ZED

Ms/Mrs/Miss/Mr ....Initials ....

BLOCK CAPITALS PLEASE

Surname ....

Address ....

....

....Postcode ....

Send this whole page to:
UK: FREEPOST CN81, Croydon, CR9 3WZ
EIRE: PO Box 4546, Kilcock, County Kildare (stamp required)

Offer valid in UK and Eire only and not available to current Reader Service subscribers to this series. We reserve the right to refuse an application and applicants must be aged 18 years or over. Only one application per household. Terms and prices subject to change without notice. Offer expires 30th September 2003. As a result of this application, you may receive offers from Harlequin Mills & Boon and other carefully selected companies. If you would prefer not to share in this opportunity please write to The Data Manager at the address above.

Mills & Boon® is a registered trademark owned by Harlequin Mills & Boon Limited.
Medical Romance™ is being used as a trademark.